Wasted on the Young

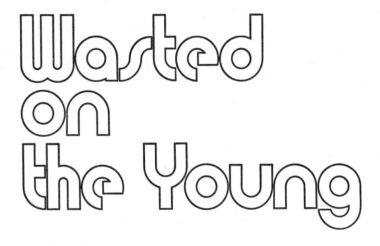

Wasted on the Young

Ralph Schoenstein

THE BOBBS-MERRILL COMPANY, INC.
Indianapolis, New York

For Arthur Hershkowitz,
with increasing admiration

If only when one heard
That old age was coming,
One could bolt the door
And refuse to meet him.

Kokinshu
Japanese poet

I wouldn't be 18 again
for anything in the world.

Loving Care
American rinse

He began to rub his hand on the back of her blouse.

"Wait a minute," she said, suddenly pulling back. "I know what you're doing; I've read about this. You're trying to unhook my bra."

"No—no, really," he quickly said. "I was just . . . admiring your vertebrae; they're very cute. They're graduated like a good set of pearls."

"Jesus, I haven't worn a bra since I left St. Cecelia's—and even that one didn't hook. How old are you, anyway?"

"Who, me? Why . . . thirty-two."

"Oh, come on, hooked bras and graduated pearls have been out for a hundred years."

He leaned back a bit on the couch, his lust giving way to disgust, and manufactured a laugh while she studied his boyish face and his thinning hair.

"I'll bet you're close to forty," she said. "Funny, you don't really look like such an elderly man."

Wasted on the Young

He had reached the point where he was thinking of suicide, but that involved a certain risk: the insurance men might refuse to pay his two beneficiaries, a mother of sixty-nine and a father of seventy-one, who could have used the money to make themselves fifty-five or -six at Sarasota's new Counter-geriatrics Inn. But if he did decide to self-destruct, he would have to do it before June 19 so his obituary would still be able to report those golden words, "Mr. Stone was thirty-nine." The rest of the obituary, run not in the *Times* but in the *Amherst Alumni Review*, would be a decided anticlimax to his age:

Mr. Stone, a research chemist for Pavlov Pet Cuisine ("We make 'em salivate"), spent the last fifteen years helping his company find methods to put less of the food in the can. He leaves a father, mother, and brother, endless mental copulations with Kathryn Grayson and Jeanne Crain, and an absolute dread of being forty.

His brother, by the way, happens to be the successful one. A full thirteen years younger than the late obscure Randall Stone, G. Arnold Stone produces both "The Ovary Game" and "The Bereavement Game" for ABC. He is also a member of the Committee on Packaging of the President's Council on the Arts.

He got out of bed and took a cigarette, which didn't help because he didn't smoke; and so he turned once again to that tranquilizer called the past, trying to hide in the movies he had seen when he was twelve. But the present kept pouring over him like the shower in the next apartment, which rained on Sinatra's singing of "Sunday, Monday, or Always." Then he tuned his mental Sinatra to "I'll Get By," but a dog down the hall began barking counterpoint; and moments later, in the apartment above, there were the thumps, scratches, and skids of a dog that was either having a breakdown or trying to learn to play hockey. How fitting that New York's dogs were romping with him on his trip to the brink, because he had wasted the prime of his life at Pavlov's Pet Cuisine, where he was also working on a food that would make a dog feel hungry shortly after a meal.

What a pathetic case, he thought: a man lost in the past, losing to the present, and terrified of the future, a man whom the youth takeover was pushing toward the prune juice of Miami Beach, where his parents already lived, comparing transplants and grandchildren with other senior old people. Randy was a junior old person, a lost son of the Eisenhower years who had silently peaked between Bobby Thomson's homer and the sinking of the *Andrea Doria.* Why, he wondered, hadn't *his* generation conquered America with a tyranny of youth? Why hadn't *they* taken charge at twenty-three, when all the cops and quarterbacks still looked like authentic men? Why hadn't he and all of the other contemporaneous quiet bloomers done something to get themselves deified instead of just sitting around in charcoal grays admiring Willie Mays? Well, at least he'd be going out with a bang, like Hemingway. Too bad he couldn't use the suicide to promote a book. Unfortunately, he'd be plugging Pavlov Cuisine, for he planned to do it in the lab, where he would make this final dropout an eloquent cry for a national sense of proportion: Americans spent more on dog food than on medical research, in which Randall Sydney Stone once had dreamed of spending his life as the distinguished and often laid friend of Donna Reed.

Although it was almost midnight, he left his bed and began to dress, pausing for a moment to look again at the latest correspondence from his dear old maddening mother.

Randy Sweet,

Many thanks for another very thoughtful shipment of Pavlov. If your father and I ever do get a dog, he'll be the best fed one on the Beach. Of course no better than the way I always fed you. And he could never be any more loyal.

Randy dear, it just occurred to me that you'll be forty this summer, which means you're not getting any younger. Is there something wrong? We see David Susskind down here, so if you're homosexual or something else we'll understand. Otherwise your father and I would love to have some pictures of grandchildren to show at the shuffleboard. When the others start showing grandchildren, all we can do is fight back with your report cards, which they've already seen. I know you go out with lots of girls, but your father says that might just be a cover.

Our whole gang sends their love. Gertrude is going on 73 but passing as 60, Ceil is still only 69 but looks 104, and half of Rose looks 55 and half looks 90. She had a nose transplant that's taking beautifully but her torso work was kind of botched. She had a breast rotation by a local man and he turned them the wrong way. They're doing such wonderful things these days, but not on Rose. Still, who can be perfect with a science so new? It's thrilling to know that no one ever has to get old if you have a big enough man! But you definitely can't renovate on Medicare.

Your father and I would still like to go to that Countergeriatrics Inn at Sarasota where they gave Sam a whole new neck. Your father says that more of these clinics are opening all the time, so we'll just have to wait for a Korvette's. Do you happen to know the most years they've ever taken off anybody? Not that we want the record, but it *would* be fun to be the same age as you.

Keep doing good work with the dogs, but get serious about a girl if you can.

Love,   Mother

Randy crunched up the letter in disgust. His mother's obsession with youth was even more depressing than his own realization that he had already been forty for fifteen years. Mindlessly he turned on the television set in the hope of getting one goodbye look at Donna or Jeanne; but instead of the midnight movie, there was the climax of "Miss Pre-Teen America," a pageant produced by G. Arnold Stone, a perfectly American success at twenty-six, who had peaked at twenty-three with "The Ovary Game" and was now racing along toward the twilight of his career. On the screen Randy saw the last of the finalists declaim to a hushed audience what menstruation would mean to her.

"If I am allowed to menstruate," she said with a voice fit for a period that began on the Fourth of July, "it will mean that I will be allowed to take my place beside millions of other women of twelve and one-half who are helping to shape America. And America is surely the greatest land in the world, not just for *having* a cycle but for *re*cycling too. Thank you."

And then, while the judges made their choice, the show had an interview with twenty-five-year-old Harold Wren, the newly elected United States senator from Tennessee, who made a brief inspirational statement about how he would be spending the four and one-half years before he was allowed to receive the oath of office.

"I am not in favor of lowering the voting age to twelve," he finally said, "unless such a citizen is fully aware of the functions of government and is also not wetting the bed."

The show then cut to a promotion for a new evening series called "The Young Colonials," in which the American Revolution was the doing of their own thing by some Philadelphia dropouts. Needless to say, Randy thought, the seventy-year-old Benjamin Franklin would be only a doty optician. Thank God he wouldn't be around to see the shows of seasons to come, to see "The Young Civil Warriors," in which a bewildered Ulysses Grant was briefed at a day care center near Richmond.

He finished dressing and turned off the set as a promotion began for Morty Sneed, the six-year-old who had just been hired by Channel 9 to cover children's news as America's most cuddly correspondent, a kind of eyewitness runt. Starting for the door, Randy suddenly asked himself: At thirty-nine and three-quarters, am I really over the hill? *No,* goddam it; it was just that the hill had been moved.

Two

When Camus said that the only philosophical problem was suicide, he was obviously brooding about how to make a poetic departure in a dog food testing lab. Randy wondered if he should turn to Pavlov's new cosmetic line and try to dispatch himself by drinking some FDS, Fido's Daintiest Scent, "for the dog that wants to feel feminine again after being spayed." He wondered if anyone would get the symbolism of such a death, since he didn't quite get it himself. He had better do some explaining in the note that he would be leaving to help his parents get through their twenty-five years of mourning; but they didn't really need him, of course: they could always *adopt* some grandchildren, and their Arnie was certainly success enough for two. They could stop showing

Randy's report cards and concentrate on having parties to enjoy "The Ovary Game." They must have been especially proud during this week's show, an all-time high in the ratings because of the dramatic victory of Pregnancy Number Three. She'd come in as an underdog because she had just turned twelve and there were doubts about her womb; in fact, cycle fans in the studio audience had been crying "Get a rabbit!"; but then Dr. Jerry, the genial gynecologist, had come out and announced that she was truly two months gone, and all America sighed.

He grabbed a sheet of paper and began to write:

Dear Mom and Dad:

In case you're upset by my suicide, there's something I want you to keep in mind: you have one son who's a fantastic success, and no parents can ever expect to bat more than .500 in the reproduction league.

You see, it's all so hopeless for me. The parade has passed me by, and I don't want to wait until I'm replaced by a junior high school dropout. I keep getting older every day, which is the worst mistake you can make in America today. I'm so tired of going downhill in a world that's run by juvenile

And then he stopped writing, suddenly startled by a barking from Rhonda, the arthritic old beagle he was planning to use for a test of Pavlov's new aphrodisiac, a dinner treat for aging hounds that wanted one last crack at heat. Randy hurried across the lab and saw that Rhonda was running around her cage with a spryness that astounded him, for her first experimental treatment was still a couple of weeks away. It was to be done as part of a pilot for Arnie's new show, "The Pet Game," in which contestants would try to win for their cats and dogs a weekend of fornication in Acapulco or Cannes. As he stood there in wonderment, Randy noticed a puddle inside

the cage that Rhonda was lapping at, a puddle far from her
water bowl that seemed to have come either from some kind
of leak or a mouse with a kidney condition; but then he saw on
a shelf above him the broken pieces of a bottle of testrogen,
the aphrodisiac that was a blend of testosterone, estrogen,
and Schweppes; and overturned just beside it was a can of
Ovaltine, whose powder had been mixed with the testrogen as
it had flowed from the shelf to the cage. Was this the work of
an industrial spy who was seeking a chocolaty road to
erection? The testrogen was still a secret, and even the
Ovaltine label said "based on an original Swiss formula."

No matter what had caused this spillage, the important thing
was that a thirteen-year-old hound had miraculously lost her
arthritis. In fact, she was acting so frisky that she actually
seemed to be younger. The scene was a shaggy Lourdes; but
neither Randy nor Rhonda was Catholic, so the explanation
lay in biochemistry. The testrogen was intended to trigger just
a little twilight lust, and the Ovaltine's basic function was for
Randy's coffee breaks. Ovaltine, with every single vitamin a
child should have. Ovaltine, the early morning edge for the
American fighting man in his conquest of the beery Nazis and
the tea-soaked Nipponese. Ovaltine . . . for a moment Randy's mind, that swamp of retrospection, slipped back again
into the past, back to Ovaltine's radio hero, Captain Midnight,
who was no teenage hash-happy drummer but a valiant
middle-aged bore. In *those* days teenagers were merely the
sidekicks who fetched ammo and Mallomars for the vigorously
mature crime fighters of forty-two.

But return with us now, he thought, to the thrilling moment
at hand, when Randy's present suddenly seemed worthwhile.
What, he wondered, would happen if he gave Rhonda another
dose of this incredible stuff? The scientist in him, which was
second rate, said go ahead, and so he prepared another dish

of the yummy elixir, put it inside the cage, and watched
Rhonda take it all. At once she started barking and bounding
about like a frisky pup; but only moments later she lay down
and went to sleep, dreaming no doubt of advances by
Dobermans, German shepherds, and perhaps even elephants.
And then it dawned on Randy that Rhonda wasn't asleep, she
was dead: he had given her an overdose. His feel for failure
had triumphed again. He felt very tired right now, so he threw
himself down on a cot beside the wall, deciding that he'd do a
better job of ending things when he was refreshed.

When he was awakened by Rhonda's barking six hours
later, the lab was full of sun but the cage was less full of
Rhonda: she was actually *smaller*; and he also saw evidence
of the first time that she had ever lost bowel control at night.
Was this her opinion of the experiment, or had she regressed
to being pre-toilet-trained? It was the latter, he decided,
suddenly seeing the positive side of things. Rhonda's rejuvenation had inspired one in him: he had gone to sleep as a
middle-aged depressive and awakened as a young optimist.
He suddenly envisioned a lovely late-blooming life that could
go on past June 19, and his dread of that date was gone. Why,
when the *Pope* was thirty-nine, he still hadn't done a thing,
while Randy now was savoring an achievement even greater
than being able to recite all the names of the Seven Dwarfs.

He quickly opened the cage and let the diminished Rhonda
start to romp about the lab. His mind reeled with elation as he
beheld a formerly arthritic old animal that somehow had
recaptured its youth. Randy had stumbled on the Fountain of
Puppyhood.

"God *damn!*" he cried joyously, and he knew the exhilara-
tion of Newton discovering gravity, of Stanley discovering
Livingstone, of Hefner discovering breasts.

It was a scientific miracle, no doubt—somewhat short on

controls, of course, but he still could see no other conclusion: a mixture of testrogen and Ovaltine had made a thirteen-year-old beagle travel most of the way back to the womb. The stuffy old Nobel Committee would want all kinds of traditional proof, but the aging Randy had no time to take four or five thousand hounds and give half of them the elixir and the other half Nestlé's Quik. He was salivating, fittingly enough, at the thought of leaving dogs and trying the elixir on a lower form, human beings. Should he try it first on *himself?* He would be honored even more as the *teenage* inventor of the world's first rejuvenator. However, there was always the chance that he might give himself too much, and as a child he wouldn't be able to carry on the work. The elixir was something fierce: Rhonda had gone all the way back to one or two after just a puddle and a dish of—what should he call it? Testrogine, of course. He picked up a pen and quickly wrote out the formula: *equal parts of testrogen, Ovaltine and Schweppes mixed in a dirty bowl.* Then he put Rhonda back in the cage and let out another cry of jubilation, like the ones that must have come from Christopher Columbus, age forty-*one.* And then Randy Stone, who had finally made it when he was safely thirty-nine, went off to find a human being to test the greatest invention since the wheel. Hell, he decided, the wheel would have made it on its own.

Three

The Countergeriatrics Inn at Lake Bluff, Illinois, based on Dr. Paul Niehans's Clinique La Prairie, was one of three American clinics where people were rejuvenated with cells from the fetuses of slaughtered lambs; and for those who also wanted more traditional doses of youth, à la carte hormone shots were given too. The Lake Bluff clinic catered mostly to those who had spent their lives trying to meet Merle Oberon, while the one in Sarasota handled aging canasta players and the one in Beverly Hills recycled film stars of over fifty and rock musicians of thirty-one. Each clinic was a cross between a hospital and a hotel, with all the gaiety of a hospital and the medical facilities of a hotel; the average patient stayed there a week for thirteen hundred dollars. This fee was tax deductible because Congress had finally decided that rejuvenation was as basic to the good life in America as antirubella shots. The Sarasota clinic was slightly more expensive than the other two because it had a sauna for those who wanted to lose as many pounds as years. "Come here a fat alter cocker," its handsome brochure said, "and go home a skinny kid."

The director of the Lake Bluff Countergeriatrics Inn, Dr. Reuben Rogers, was a blond and deeply tanned man of fifty-five whose real name, Klaus von Stahl, had been with him during the years that he had been dabbling listlessly in dermatology. But when he drifted into sexual therapy and suddenly came alive, he changed his name, briefly considering Rogers Reuben and then deciding that Reuben Rogers had a nicer Episcopal ring. For three and one-half years he wrote a weekly newspaper column of tips on how to make love that was full of adorable plays on tennis and sex like "How to come to net" and "Avoiding a double fault." He was about to leave the newspaper and offer the column to *Sports Illustrated* when he was struck by the thought that many ten-year-olds knew as much about sex as he did and some of them knew more. Such a moment of truth would have sent a less resourceful man back to probing the wonders of acne, but Rogers's resources happened to be considerable, for they had come from the lively sale of his textbook, *Sing, Vagina*; and so he redirected his career away from the growing mob in sexual therapy and into the much more fashionable rejuvenation game. When *Sing, Vagina* was made supplemental reading in the Minneapolis public school system, the profit enabled Rogers to open the Lake Bluff Countergeriatrics Inn.

As Randy entered the Inn, he heard the strains of "You Make Me Feel So Young" coming from speakers that suddenly switched to an urgent voice, "Fetal alert. Fetal alert. Clear all halls and ready all rejuvenees." In some of the open rooms that Randy was passing, he saw the buttocks of Beautiful People who were awaiting the blessed needle, for the shot had to be given as soon as possible after the killing of what had become the replacement for the Lamb of God.

What a silly old pagan procedure, Randy thought, but what a revolution he was about to start. Fetal extract shots were merely a holding action against old age, a way to keep someone looking fifty for another few fearful years; but to reverse the body's clock and start it back the other way, to set up in the body a kind of teenage saving time, was a breakthrough that would alter the course of humanity.

When Randy walked into Rogers's office, the doctor was busy hitting a tennis ball against the opposite wall, but he graciously stopped and turned to his visitor.

"What can I do for you?" he said in a voice that was pure petroleum.

"Doctor, I'm Randall Stone, a research chemist with Pavlov Pet Cuisine, and what I'm about to say to you may sound a little strange, but I'd like to borrow one of your patients."

"You want to make a referral deal?"

"No, I want to test a rejuvenation method that I think will go far beyond Niehans. You may not believe this, but I've already succeeded in reducing a beagle from thirteen years old to *two.*"

"There isn't much market for beagle reduction," Rogers said. "It's *people* who can't stand age."

"I know: I have a mother. I also have myself. And a couple of days ago I was ready for suicide because I'm almost forty."

"Yes, we're getting more and more suicidal thirty-nines—a nice little twist on the old Jack Benny joke. So how the hell did you get that dog all the way down to two?"

"Well, I really shouldn't tell you, but if you'll lend me a patient, I'll give you half the formula right now and the other half when it works."

This was publishing talk that Rogers understood.

"That makes sense," he said, "but why should I help the competition?"

"Because all scientists are brothers," Randy replied.

Although Rogers was always delighted to be taken for a scientist, he still was not convinced.

"I dunno . . ." he said, thoughtfully tossing a Wilson three-dot into the air. "Speaking strictly as a scientist, I have to remind you that youth is big business now—we're even trying to get it listed on the American Exchange—and I'm not so sure that a dog food man would fit on the team. And suppose I gave you a patient and you killed him? I'd not only lose his fee but I'd also have plenty of trouble with the malpractice insurance boys—unless I could first work out some kind of one-patient deductible. No, Mr. Stone, I think that cellular therapy is just about as far as the youth industry should go."

"But what about that man in the Bahamas who's trying new things with eggs?"

"Yeah, he has 'em swallow live chicken embryos along with the minced lamb shots, but the cholesterol in those chicks just makes you a younger artery case. He's fooling around with some other concoctions too, but the point is why look for trouble with rhino horn and newt's nuts and shit like that when lamb cells and hormones have already been proved to knock off a full ten years?"

"Is *that* the American way?" said Randy angrily. "To settle for a lousy ten years? Why, right now in China and Russia they're probably working on ways to knock off thirty or *forty*, which is just what I think *I* can do."

"No, they like 'em old in China. The Russians could probably start something to get back for our taking the moon, but right now there really isn't much of a rejuvenation gap. Just that clinic in Rumania, but the AMA won't recognize it."

"It's still going for thirty, I'll bet. What's the technique?"

"An intravenous anesthetic—procaine—but you have to take it for years; and it wouldn't work over here anyway. Americans can only spare a week or two to rejuvenate. Look, I'd still like to know this technique of yours."

Feeling as though he were fighting for his life, Randy decided to try to lure Rogers into the deal by teasing him with half of the formula, the more sensational half.

"Okay, I'll tell you this much," he said. "It involves the use of Schweppes and Ovaltine."

Rogers emitted a soft reverent whistle and let his ball fall to the court.

"Schweppes and Ovaltine . . . of *course!* What a blend of refreshment and power! It was there all the time and none of us ever saw it because we were so wrapped up in testicles. Schweppes and Ovaltine, of *course.*"

"The Russians are probably trying club soda and Cocoa Marsh," Randy said, "but this is something *atomic.*"

"It's genius."

"And that's only half of it."

"You don't even *need* the other half."

"So isn't there just *one* patient in this whole place who might want to go beyond lamb cells and hormone shots?"

"Well now, lemme see . . ."

Rogers thought of his current guests, quickly reviewing the desperation of each: one balding congressman about to be opposed by a Harvard graduate student; six fading actresses who were fighting to avoid being claimed by horror films; three slightly sagging heiresses who were currently sleeping with a cabin boy, a beach boy, and a ball boy; five executives who were nervously nearing the retirement age of forty-three; and twenty-eight rather contented prostitutes.

And then he remembered her.

"Saralee Kravitz," he said.

"Saralee *Kravitz?*" said Randy in disbelief. "*Cupcake* Kravitz, the senator's wife? The one who can always get a table at Maxine's . . . is *here?*"

Rogers allowed himself a bit of a smile and said, "I don't deal in welfare cases."

"You sure don't. Cupcake Kravitz and Cardinal Cooke are the only two people who have never been known to get fuck-you's from Maxine."

"She's here, all right, but not under her own name, of course; she's using Emily Dickinson. That's partly because the senator's here too and neither one has told the other. You see, they're in kind of a race to get back to thirty-five again, and the senator's hair transplant has put real pressure on Saralee: she keeps asking for something stronger than sheep. Yes, I think that she's your girl."

Randy's heart was racing now. Not only did he have a potential subject for his historic test, but he had one who resembled Rita Hayworth, the very first girl of his boyhood wet dreams.

"When can I see her?" he said.

Four

Because of face lifts, transplants, implants, and supplementations, Saralee and Sidney Kravitz were continuously revising the age difference between them. At the time that she left for the Lake Bluff Countergeriatrics Inn, Saralee was chronologically nine years younger than the senator's sixty-six, but he was closing in fast from above because his hair transplant had taken so well that it was making a bold descent down his forehead, giving him a boyishly simian look and putting pressure on Saralee to have some other part of her tightened, raised, or lubed. Her first face-lift had been surgical, but the five after that had been silicone shots from one of the portable kits that a famous Italian princess was seductively selling in televised song:

All alone
With my silicone
But no longer feeling blue,
'Cause my wrinkled face
I will soon erase
And my sagging neck
Will be in check
Too.

While dressing recently for an evening at Maxine's, Saralee
had been tempted to take another silicone booster to reestab-
lish total tautness in her chin, remove a small emerging line
southwest of her nose, and reverse some potential slippage
under her eyes; but a yawn that she wasn't completely able to
make convinced her that perhaps she had tuned her face as
much as she could without supervision; and so she had left for
Lake Bluff as the next event in the epidermal Olympics that
she and Sidney were having. She had told him in a long
distance call that she was going away to do some fund raising
for her latest noble cause: fighting a new strain of Chicano
gonorrhea with an organization that she affectionately called
Clap Trap. Since Sidney spent most of his time in Washington,
she really didn't have to tell him anything at all, for they had
the kind of marriage in which a week's disappearance was
never noticed. Had they accidentally met at the Inn, it would
have been the kind of meeting that sometimes took place in
their New York apartment.

Although they clearly weren't Tristan and Isolde, Sidney and
Saralee did share two great common bonds: the desire to see
him become the first Jewish President and the hobby of
having affairs with editors of magazines. Sidney was currently
dallying with Dora Dooley Hatch, editor of *Go, Girl, Go!*, and
Saralee, who also had dallied with Dora Dooley Hatch, was
currently spending her free time under Roger Blackman,

editor of *Manhattan Muckraker*. Blackman had settled down
on top of Saralee not just because she resembled Rita
Hayworth but also because she was the queen of New York's
Beautiful People and the North American rival of Merle
Oberon. She had, in fact, been learning Spanish from her
building's Nicaraguan handyman, who also taught her an act
he once had done for American tourists.

This remarkable social leader, this lover of both the mighty
and the unfortunate, had come to New York thirty years ago
from Lima, Ohio, the daughter of a simple seamstress and a
numbers executive, and at once had devoted herself to giving
parties, luring celebrities to her big apartment with the
promise of meeting other celebrities similarly lured. Her most
triumphant double lure had been playing off Albert Schweit-
zer's daughter with Mussolini's son, an encounter she
launched by saying, "Both your fathers started things in
Africa, so you two should have so much to talk about." By the
time she had become the city's best known hostess, the birth
of a baking company had inspired Saralee's friends to
nickname her Cupcake, although her enemies said that
Wonder was a more fitting company because her major talent
was simulating achievement: she always seemed to be starting vaguely worthy projects—like bringing back the passen-
ger pigeon—and then losing interest in them because of an
attention span that belonged in a child. Some of these
projects were conceived during evenings at Maxine's, the
noisy little East Side pub where celebrities fought for the
honor of being insulted by a glamorous former wrestler from
Washington Heights.

When Reuben Rogers introduced Randy and Saralee, she
was lying under some upper Amazon mud that she had
imported to defend her skin until she could open her mouth

wide enough to return to silicone. Even in this condition, she still appeared to the excited Randy as a mucky Rita Hayworth, an encrusted invitation to nostalgia and lust. Rogers already had told her that Randy might be the Columbus of rejuvenation, so that when he arrived in her room she smiled at him warmly through the mud.

"I'll leave you two alone," Rogers said, "and go off to tend my sheep; but let me know what's happening. And of course, Mrs. Kravitz, any extra results won't go on your bill."

For several seconds after Rogers had left the room, Randy nervously wondered about the next thing he should say, for Saralee Kravitz was the second most famous person he had ever met, falling just behind Captain Kangaroo, who once had passed through a dog show for Pavlov Pet Cuisine. But the IQ that had turned out all those report cards for his mother was never dormant long, and finally Randy said, "This is probably an idiotic question—in fact, drop the probably—but did anyone ever tell you that you look like Rita Hayworth?"

"Yes, Rita told me," Saralee said, "and a couple of million others, but most of them think she's an older version of me."

She spoke very quickly, in a throaty baritone, and Randy found himself wondering exactly what movie her voice was coming from.

"Do you . . . come here often?" he said, trying to snap himself back to the momentous business at hand.

"First time," she said. "I was thinking of trying that clinic in Rumania, but I don't like the idea of using anesthetic—propane or something. It's so terribly important for one to stay sensitive, to be vital and perceptive, don't you think? Also, no one is going to Rumania this year. Now tell me about this miracle of yours: you tried it first on a *dog?* What breed?"

"A beagle, unpedigreed, but she really tried it on herself: it was an accident."

"And she actually got *younger?*"

"By several years; it was incredible. She went from thirteen to acting like one or two."

"Now wait, let me figure that out. . . . One dog year equals . . . Why, I'd lose eighty or ninety *years;* I'd be a positive *embryo* again!" She laughed huskily. "Wouldn't *that* be one for Leonard Lyons."

"Mrs. Kravitz, how old are you?—if I may ask."

"Fifty-seven and a fifth."

"You look about forty-six—that is, the parts that I can see."

"Yes, but that's about as far as I can go with silicone, hormones, mud, and sheep. I just can't seem to make it back to forty, where they say life begins."

"The man who said that was a schmuck: he must have been thinking of life in Korea. It's down around twelve in America today."

"Jesus, how true, how true. Now tell me honestly, Dr. Stone—"

"It's *Mister* Stone."

"Good, I don't trust doctors—except Rogers, of course, but he doesn't really know that much medicine and he's such an utterly charming man. Tell me honestly now, just how far back do you think you can get me?"

"Oh, gosh," Randy said, "I couldn't begin to guess; this is all so damned experimental. But if you have anything in common with that beagle, there's an outside chance that . . . well, I just might be able to make you twenty-one again."

"Fan*tas*tic!"

"That's the ideal result, of course. We could also hit thirty or forty or fifty—"

"That's where I am *now.*"

"—or nothing."

"There's no chance of a *back*fire, is there?" she said

anxiously. "I mean, you're sure it's pointed in the right *direction?*"

Randy smiled. "Oh, no chance of that. Even if the formula fails, it'll be a great little pickup. But tell me, why are you so desperate to look even younger than you already do?"

"Mr. Stone, do you know who my husband is?"

"Of course."

"Then you also know that the Senate isn't necessarily the end of the line. One of these days the presidency will be going to a token Jew, and that token can be Sidney Kravitz. Now I'm sure that you've noticed how much younger he's been looking lately: he's made a marvelous backward move. Well, *I* have to keep up the pace because the voters certainly won't go for a young man with a matronly wife. So rejuvenation has become the game that Sidney and I are playing on his way to the White House. You see, youth rules the world, Mr. Stone. It's the one thing you should teach your children to hold on to."

"I have no children, but when I do, you can bet I'll let them know what they've got."

"Your experiment also appeals to me because it sounds like a total job. Princess Peggy paid two thousand dollars just to have her ass lifted last month, but I'm tired of things like that; it's piecemeal work. A buttocks here, a bosom there, a nose, a neck, a hank of hair—I want it all at once. Now what's your formula for getting it?"

"I'd really rather not say," Randy told her uneasily. "It's sort of classified . . . if you know what I mean."

"Oh, come *on* now, sweetie," she said, reaching up and touching his cheek with her muddy hand. "I've been keeping secrets for years. Men in the Pentagon have told me things that even *Congress* never knew, but you didn't see me go blabbing them to the House Armed Services Committee." She pressed his cheek.

"Well . . . okay, it's got hormones and Ovaltine and Schweppes—but I can't tell you in what combination."

"Ovaltine and Schweppes—fantastic! The Fountain of Youth is a two cents plain!"

Randy laughed. "It's already been a tonic for me. In fact, it saved my life."

"*Your* life?"

"Uh huh. A couple of days ago, I was about to end it all and let my mother collect the insurance."

"Yes, sometimes the thought of suicide is the only real comfort we have. You aren't married?"

"I've never found the right one. Maybe I've spent too much time with my stupid work; maybe I'm too much of a dreamer, I don't know. At any rate, the ideal rela—oh, hell, let's just say that I've never found what you and Sidney have."

"Yes, we have it, but not with each other. But that's another story." She sat up and wiped the mud from her face. "All right, my young genius, when do we reverse me? . . . What are you staring at?"

"I'm sorry, it's just that the resemblance is uncanny. There was a forties musical where Rita . . . If only I'd met you when you were younger."

"Maybe you will, maybe you will."

Early that evening, while Randy was preparing the Testro-gine for Saralee, his comrades in rejuvenation were at work all over the world in their ageless struggle to wipe out age, to rescue mankind's precious carcasses from the ravages of time, to give to humanity lovelier skin, merrier blood, sturdier muscles, and ejaculations.

At a clinic in Johannesburg, the disciples of Dr. Max Wolf, father of the internal rebirth plan, were brewing their yeast protein to regenerate the vital organs of patients who believed in a fermented Fountain of Youth.

At a clinic in Honolulu, the disciples of Dr. Ivan Popov,

father of the placental extract plan, were about to abort an expectant ewe, clinging to their faith in rebirth through afterbirth.

At a clinic in Bucharest, the disciples of Dr. Ana Aslan, mother of Gerovital, the popular name for the procaine compound KH-3, were about to start servicing a Swedish painter of eighty-four who had recently fallen in love.

At a clinic in the Bahamas, other disciples of Ana Aslan were hedging their bets on KH-3 by also having their patients swallow live chick embryos; and a kindergarten teacher from Shaker Heights was also hedging her bet on the chicks with heaping side dishes of yogurt.

At a clinic in Switzerland, the disciples of Dr. Paul Niehans, father of cell therapy, were grinding their fetal lambs while wondering how to murder Dr. Reuben Rogers.

At a clinic in Kiev, the disciples of all the above were examining a Georgian gentleman of one hundred and twenty-six, who was wondering what could be done to improve his sexual life.

And at a clinic in Los Angeles, the disciples of no one in particular were preparing to peel the face, lift the thighs, and relocate the chin of a regular patient whose navel would soon be her only original part.

But all this accumulated medical acumen was about to become medieval as Randy headed for Saralee's room with a smile and a syringe.

Saralee had fallen asleep a few minutes after the injection of Testrogine. She had almost passed out a few minutes before it when she learned that Randy had never given an injection to anything higher than a very bright basset hound; but he had calmed her nerves by saying that he recently had seen a documentary on dope addiction and could easily handle the shot.

It was now almost thirty minutes after he had plunged his pioneering syringe into Saralee's brave behind, and he was still standing over her, anxiously seeking the first faint signs of fifty or forty-five. Rhonda's rejuvenation had taken from midnight till dawn, but Saralee's should have been faster because she had a desire that the beagle clearly lacked. Now, however, as he looked down upon her, she was still just an over-renovated fifty-seven and a fifth.

Finally he walked away, sank into the sofa on the other side of the room, let his eyelids close, and began to think about age, the only thing he'd been thinking about since the day of Rhonda's great retreat.

Grow old along with me, the best is yet to be, the last of life, like thirty-eight or nine . . . Vitamin E is very big right now with a lot of the rejuvenating crowd. Should I have used it to buffer the Schweppes? . . . A man is only as old as his connective tissue, says Bogomolets. Will Testrogine go directly to all of Saralee's decaying little links? Or will it be detoured into her liver and spleen? . . . Then younger than springtime am I, gayer than hormones am I, fresher than any fetus of sheep am I . . .

And then he fell asleep.

He was jolted awake by Saralee, who was brandishing a mirror and a face full of ecstasy.

"It's *worked,* it's *worked!*" she cried, embracing Randy so that he felt the full rubbery richness of her breasts. "Just *look* at me: I'm *resurrected!* I'm forty-three if I'm a *day* and you're a *genius,* you beautiful man!"

And then she began to dance around the room, singing:

You made me feel so young,
Da-da-de-da-da-dung-dung-dung.

Resurrected was a fitting word, for the pirouetting figure that Randy saw as he came fully awake made him feel like a witness to a Biblical miracle. Saralee's rejuvenation was no mere tightening of the old epidermal drum: it was an age reduction from within: her eyes were shining, her muscles had spring and grace, and the hardness was gone from her face. Her skin was still taut, of course, but she could now fully open her mouth, as she was doing in manic song.

He had been half in love with her before, and now he completed the trip: he was suddenly seized by a desire to take her home and marry her, even if such a wedding would postpone a Jewish presidency; for no creator who ever lived, from Pygmalion to Mattel, could have felt about his master-piece the way Randy now felt about Saralee. The Testrogine had reduced her fifteen years and had given him the girl of his dreams, the kind they weren't making anymore, except in this room at the Inn.

"Hallelujah!" he announced, and he jumped from his chair and started dancing with Saralee in what seemed to be a blend of a tarantella and a waltz.

"La-da-da-dee . . . la-da-da-dee," she sang to the music sounding in her brain, her private rite of spring.

"Mrs. Kravitz, we *did* it!" he cried, triumphantly stomping a few of her toes. "It's a ninety percent new you!"

"Darling, call me *Saralee*—or *Cupcake*—or Tart—or—oh, I just can't *tell* you how I feel! Just *wait* till they see me at Maxine's! That bitch'll have to get lighting now! And Sidney . . . oh, Sidney, I'll be your Jackie Kennedy now!"

"And wait till my mother tells her gang about this!" Randy said as they continued their euphoric stumble around the room. "Your *body* . . . your *face* . . ."

He was starting to lose his breath, but he wasn't inclined to end his envelopment of her insufficient nightie.

"Yes, just *look* at that ass!" she said. "I *never* thought I'd see it again—as firm as that summer at Cannes!" And then she sang:

> *I'm just a kid again,*
> *Hit me with some id again . . .*

"Hey, slow down; I'm winded . . . I'm not as young as you."

Saralee merrily spun him onto the bed, where he found himself wondering if Edison, Franklin, and Bell had enjoyed erections at their moments of success.

"Why, *sweetie,* you're just a *boy.*"

And before he could say What hath God wrought? she began a new rhythm with her loins and was making it with her maker. He had always been an ejaculator slower only than a chimpanzee, so this was a fleeting moment indeed.

"Thank you," he said, instantly hating himself for what well might have been a definitively dumb remark.

"Thank *you,*" said Saralee, "for the new equipment. It hasn't worked like that in a dog's age." She laughed. "Hey, a *dog's* age: *that's* really what brought us together."

She laughed again; and then she sat up, grabbed her mirror, and began to adore her face, while Randy tried to collect himself, for both his body and his mind were running amuck on different planes.

"When can I take another shot?" she said.

"Now wait a minute—just *wait* a minute," he said. "This is the biggest thing since the *wheel,* and I've just got to catch my breath and get on top of it and calmly figure out where we go from here."

"Why, back to New York, of course; right away."

"Yes, back to New York. Together."

And he suddenly moved himself toward her and gave her a long wet kiss that was slightly northwest of her mouth; but she instantly centered things, opened her lips, and engaged the tongue that was about to fashion its most splendidly stupid remark.

"Saralee," he said, detaching himself a few seconds later, "will you marry me?"

"Maybe someday, sweetie," she told him, "but it would have to be after the election. I promised Sidney that I'd help make him President; and being First Lady might be fun for a while, don't you think? But there's no reason why we can't be good *friends* when I'm in the White House. Why, you'll be my personal *physician*. By the way, how often will I need the shots?"

"I don't *know;* this is all so new; I've got to think."

"I guess we have to be careful about an overdose. I mean too much of this stuff could take you right back to *infancy.*" She laughed. "Say, isn't that what everyone wants: a return to the womb? I wonder how it really *was* in the womb. I've got such a lousy memory."

Suddenly he sprang to his feet.

"The *UN!* Of *course:* the *UN.*"

"I've seen it; it's a drag. But I've never been to the Flatiron Building, and I hear—"

"I've got to *give* this thing to the UN! It's the greatest boon the human race has ever had—the Fountain of Youth at last—and I just can't give it to Helena Rubinstein!"

"Of course not: we'll start our *own* company. *You* will, I mean, and maybe I'll do a little modeling."

"No, Saralee, don't you *see:* it's just *wrong* to commercialize on something like this. This is bigger than the formula for *Coke;* and I don't want it to *be* like the formula for Coke: just stuck in some company's safe so they can make a million bucks—even if the company's *mine.* I mean Goodyear has no patent on the *wheel.* Well, this is just as big and it has to be for all mankind. Christ, I wish Arnie were here."

"With a butterfly net! A million-dollar formula is Bromo Seltzer or pizza pie: *this* one is worth *billions* and you just want to give it away to the great unwashed! Why, it'll just end up in Asia, and they don't even *want* to be young!"

"I don't agree. Did Franklin try to make a fast buck from electricity?"

"Look, Randy, *I* do charity work myself; Clap Trap is one of the biggest; but I wouldn't give them my savings account or the mortgages I hold in Bedford-Stuyvesant. If you just *give* this thing away, then everyone'll be my age and you won't have a dime to show for it. The Rumanians are making a *fortune* on Gerovital, and it's just *gumdrops* compared to this."

As he listened to her speak, he noticed that her voice was both softer and higher than it had been before, and he realized again what he had done. Saralee's rejuvenation was an incredible total thing, and he was happily terrified, both by his creation and by his falling in love with it. Did falling in love help or hinder a great scientist? Edison was always in bed alone when he took his naps, but Pierre Curie had a madame and a mistress too.

"I've got to talk to my brother Arnie," Randy said. "He has no principles, so he always knows what to do. There might be a way to use the formula to make some *money* for the UN . . . or old Navajos . . . or somebody."

"Can you trust him?"

"Of course not: he's in TV. He produces 'The Ovary Game.' "

" 'The *Ovary* Game,' I *love* it. Did you see it when that

Danish stewardess won a trip to Tahiti to tie her tubes? Okay, let's talk to your brother, your mother, your barber, *anybody*, but let's get back to New York right away. I'm *dying* for everyone to see me and I certainly don't need Rogers anymore."

"Rogers, that's right; I promised him the formula."

"Christ, I had to get myself renovated by a goddam Eagle Scout. Can't you understand that you've got to *sell* this—and for a mint. America was *built* that way."

"No, I've got to tell him; we made a deal."

"Look, Rogers sleeps till noon and *I'm* going back right away. Just give me the formula and I'll have it filled myself. If there's a problem, the drugstore'll call you."

She whipped off her nightgown to reveal the reripened fruits of Randy's labor.

"I'll fill it myself," he said. "Give me ten minutes to pack."

Shortly before noon, Reuben Rogers opened a letter that had been slipped under his door. He rubbed the sleep from his eyes and read:

Dear Dr. Rogers:

It worked! Mrs. Kravitz is on her way back, both to childhood and New York. And I'm going with her, which is why I'm not telling you in person about the full fifteen years that the formula knocked off both her outside and her inside too. The metamorphosis is beyond belief! Her clock has really been turned back, and I feel the way they must have felt when they split the atom.

I'm really sorry to rush off without saying goodbye, but Saralee is so anxious to show the senator the new her and I have to be with her to keep observing. My head is spinning around with the ramifications of this thing, which makes Gerovital seem like *gumdrops*. Saralee thinks I should commercialize on it big, but I'm going to give it to the UN—and of course to you, as I promised. You already know the first half of the formula. Well, the second half is simply equal parts of estrogen and testosterone. Just imagine: the gerontologists are doing all this wild experimenting with enzymes and the age reverser has been under our noses all along, half in puberty and half in the A&P. Now *please* keep this a secret and use it only at the Inn until the World Health Organization can get control of it. I'm afraid that people would kill to get this stuff.

I'll call you from New York and maybe we can coordinate things. With all the different formulas around, there really should be some kind of international summit meeting on rejuvenation, maybe at Disney World. I have to close now because Saralee (yes, we've gotten quite friendly since I took her down) is anxious to leave. Lord knows what's ahead for us. Youth is America's newest religion and today I feel like Jesus Christ.

> Bless you,
> Randy Stone

Rogers put down the letter and started to think, an offbeat activity for him. He had the second half of the formula now, but what the hell was the *first?* He strained to remember . . . Was it beer and Listerine? Gin and Unguentine? Cheese from the Argentine? Dammit, he'd forgotten the formula for immortality. It was just as well, he told himself: if a rejuvenator wasn't working with a little built-in senescence, he'd be putting himself out of business. Feeling better about things again, he picked up the latest copy of *The National Enquirer* and began to read about experiments in slowing the aging process by lowering the temperature of the body. Wonderful, he thought: he'd close down the Inn's heating system, which had always been an annoying expense; and he would also be able to charge his chilly guests a higher fee for the chance to go traveling down a faster highway to youth.

Six

"You're not getting older, you're getting better," the door-
man sang as they passed him on their way to Saralee's East
End apartment.

"What was he singing?" Randy asked her. "Cole Porter?"

"No, Clairol," she said. "Damn lucky that commercial's a lot
of crap or there'd be a pretty small market for Testrogine."

"I wonder if he noticed how much younger you look."

"I doubt it: he's been drunk since Christmas. We'll have to
test it on my friends, but *after* we patent it."

"I still think I should take it to the UN," he said as they
entered the self-service elevator.

"Sweetie, we *discussed* that on the plane: half the profits will *go* to the UN; and believe me, they'll be able to make millions of new teenagers in Tanzania with this dough." She moved up against him and half-whispered at his cheek, "Of course, you don't really need *me* to form a company."

"Yes I do," he said, wanting to take her right there in the elevator. If only she lived on a higher floor.

Moments later they were in her apartment, an enormous duplex he had once seen in *Town and Country* while waiting for his dentist to do a root canal. For Randy, the Beautiful People had always been tied to his rotten teeth; but now one of them was leading him right into her bedroom, where she quickly took off her jacket and everything else.

For a few seconds he gazed at the essential Saralee, wondering if she wanted a bath or him; and then he just seemed to know.

"It's not a bath you want, I presume," he said with a little smile.

Since no reply was needed, she returned the smile and then sat down beside him on her oversized double bed and started to open his shirt.

"Another test of the new equipment?" he said, trying for the kind of badinage that Saralee's bedroom seemed to demand; but the line inspired no repartee: she merely continued her silent undressing of him.

"This . . . is obviously a hobby of yours," he said. "Well, they say that sex keeps you young . . . I don't think you *needed* Testrogine."

"Let's just call this a booster," she said.

Life to Randy Stone had always seemed to be something of a dream, but there was a rich unreality to the two fantastic events that had turned his life around: discovering the Fountain of Youth and then finding a prominent nymphomaniac who was treading water there. Once again he was staggered by the thought of these two miracles that had followed the despair of his night in the Pavlov lab, when he had thought only of finding death instead of conquering it. As a middle-class child of the forties, he knew that such good fortune carried a price; and as he climbed onto Saralee, he was certain that the price was using Testrogine for humanity.

"Must you always use the missionary position?" she said.

"Who says missionaries use it?" he replied. "There's nothing in Pearl Buck about it that I—*dammit!*" His body sagged after another span of passion that was made for a chimpanzee. "I'll have to invent something to take care of that; it's a much bigger problem than aging." He made a silent vow that the next time Saralee brought him into heat—no doubt in a taxi or luncheonette—he would slow himself down by thinking of something purely nonsexual like the League of Nations or Helen Gurley Brown.

"I'm really sorry," he said.

"No apologies needed," she told him. "I happen to like you." And then she softly sang, "You made me what I am today, I hope you're satisfied."

"Oh, *I'm* satisfied, but *you're* not."

"If you made me young enough, you'd be less aroused. I bet you'd last longer if I were ten."

They both laughed, but then Randy thought of Sidney Kravitz.

"I still think I should be staying in my own apartment," he said. "There's a better class of dogs here, I know, but the senator's liable to catch us."

"Just on weekends and national holidays," she said. "The rest of the time he's in Washington with his mistress, who's a dear friend of mine. But if you really feel awkward about sharing the place with him on weekends, then of course you can go home."

"Well, he could *shoot* me, you know, and mankind would be the poorer for it."

"Worse than that, I'd be fifty-seven again."

"You're making fun of me."

"I just want you to stop your worrying and relax. This is a new life for both of us, and I don't plan to take any chances with my friendly neighborhood druggist."

"But the *senator*—"

"Could be taking us both to the White House. A triangle is America's new geometry, my friend, so stop being my little square." She turned to him and began to stroke his hair, which was thinning a bit but had only a few strands of gray. "You know, it seems to me, professor, that you're still about four or five years younger than old Saralee, so how about a few more drops of that lovely stuff to neaten up this little peer group?"

"No, I think you've had enough for a while. I mean we still don't even know if this is *dangerous*. This isn't any of your routine stuff like placentas or chickadees. I mean the government is rechecking *aspirin,* so you can bet they'll take a good look at immortality."

She placed a tender hand on his testicles. "Oh, come on, sweetie. Let's *both* take some more and try for thirty-five. Wouldn't that be a nice little downer?"

"Jesus *Christ!*" he said. "Can't you think of *anything else?* Is age the only thing anyone *thinks* about anymore? I mean that's all I *hear:* that turning forty is traumatic, that I've got the male menopause, that my brain needs a hysterectomy and my kidneys a trip to Geneva because they've been slowly disintegrating since junior high!" And then his anger drained away. "I'm sorry, Saralee . . . I don't know why that happened—yes I do: because aging is all that *I* think about too. The national disease."

"And now you've got the cure. So let's get well just a little bit more."

"No, I definitely can't take any: I'm the control." He smiled ironically. "Except I don't know what to do. . . . I've got to call Arnie and get on top of this thing."

He was thinking of his younger brother, the man he had always looked up to, when he looked up at the bedroom doorway to see Senator Sidney Kravitz, Democrat of New York, with his handball smile and his full rich head of transplant. Randy recognized Kravitz from the television news, which he could have been watching now from his position with Saralee. In fact, his first reaction was a sudden urge to change the channel.

"Jesus Christ, don't *shoot!*" he heard himself cry. "This isn't what you *think!*"

"Of course it is," said Saralee.

"Who the hell cares?" said Sidney, still smiling a bit, for it was a look that he never entirely lost.

"He won't shoot you," Saralee told Randy; "he'd lose your vote."

"Are you a registered Democrat?" Sidney asked.

"Yes," Randy replied.

"Good boy." He sat down on a chair near the bed. "Saralee, couldn't you start using Howard Johnson's for these things?"

"Then I'd keep running into you."

"Well, we really should work out a schedule for entertaining."

Now this, Randy thought, is sophistication.

"What are you doing here on a Tuesday anyway?" Saralee said.

"I came to see if I have any old position papers that might give me a new stand on capital punishment."

"Let's see. . . . You've been for it once and against it twice."

"I know, but now instead of being for it again, I'd like to find something completely new, something—" He suddenly pressed his fingertips against his contact lenses and then stared hard at Saralee. "My God, what's *happened* to you? You look like your own *daughter*."

"I have a confession to make," she said with an impish grin. "I've just come from Reuben Rogers's place."

"Well, as a matter of fact, so have *I*, but I only dropped a year or two."

She turned to Randy. "I've come with him."

"In more ways than one," Sidney said.

And then Saralee told him about the invention of Testrogine.

"Do the two of you fully appreciate what this *means?*" Sidney asked.

"It means that no one has to die until overpopulation finally kills us all," she said.

"More important than that, it means the White House for me at last!" His dyed old eyes now were wide with visions of delivering the Inaugural Address with all his original hair and teeth. "By God, that'll *do* it: I'll run as my old self: when I was thirty-eight and low in fats and had my first stand on capital punishment. Stone, if you love your country, you've got to let me take some of that stuff right away!"

"Well, I really think we should test it first," Randy said. "You might not react like Saralee."

"Well, I won't let you boff me, if that's what you mean."

"That's not nice, Sidney. The boy is in love with me, the way you used to be before you fell for yourself."

Looking embarrassed, Randy quickly said, "What I mean is that the government will want—"

"Dammit, I *am* the government, and you've got to make me

a junior senator again!" And then his face turned grave and he said half to himself, "Wait a minute now . . . Suppose people suddenly started to hold the elderly in esteem . . . No, that's strictly Chinese stuff; it couldn't happen here . . . Okay, Stone, take me down. How much of that juice is left?"

"I only made up about a pint—Reuben Rogers was short of Ovaltine—but I want to send some to my mother and father. They're seventy now and I'd like to give them fifty-five for their anniversary. But there'll be enough for everyone pretty soon because Saralee and I will be making a deal with a drug house to market it commercially, with the UN getting half the—"

"*God*, no, don't do *that*—at least not till I'm *elected!*" He looked at Randy incredulously. "You were planning to just run right out and rejuvenate the entire human race? Republicans *too?*"

"How many women of my age would you say the human race has?" Saralee said.

"Let me get this straight," Randy said, looking as morally outraged as one can when one is in bed with another man's wife. "You want the human race to wait until you become President?"

"You make it sound unreasonable," Sidney said. "A Jewish presidency will need a sacrifice or two, you know. *You* can take some, of course."

"Believe me, I'd love to pull back from the brink of forty, but I can't take a chance on dropping to twenty-one. I have to remain a mature adult and make sure that Testrogine gets out to all the senior citizens in Bangladesh."

"You know, the poor don't mind getting old," Sidney said. "I have polls to prove it. In fact, giving them a second shot at things is really a dirty trick. The nicest thing we can do for them is to help them get their lives over as quickly as possible."

This insight was lost on Randy, whose mind was wandering from Sidney's feeling for the poor because Saralee's left hand had wandered to his knee. He reached beneath the sheet and gently removed it, and then he moved slightly away from her, this creation of his who now imprisoned him in the strangest triangle since Romulus and Remus had found a place to eat. A glance at the Rita Hayworth cast of her face suddenly made him aware that he had now spent three whole days not yearning for summer evenings at the Polo Grounds or the Astor Roof. The past no longer was calling to him, but the future was even more frightening than it had been when his only fear had been turning forty.

"I think we should get something straight," he slowly said. "Testrogine isn't like the wheel, which was obviously to be used in just one way: for turning around. *This* thing . . . well, it can be used in so many different ways . . . for profit, power, vanity, or human good."

"Let's start with three out of four," said Saralee, sending her big left toe in search of the erogenous part of his shin.

"No," Randy said. "Call me an Eagle Scout if you want, but you two just can't have it all to yourselves until the election. Too many people will age in the next eight months."

"All we want is a little head start: just three or four months," she said, moving the toe northward to a warmer clime.

"Well . . . okay. But I want Testrogine in the over age nations by Labor Day."

"Good boy!" Sidney said. "You no longer have to ask what you're doing for your country." He began to remove his pants. "I presume you give it this way."

And as the semidressed senator took Randy's place in bed, Randy went to the refrigerator for his Testrogine and syringe, wondering if historians would one day call this moment the making of the President.

In his graph-lined office overlooking Third Avenue, G. Arnold Stone was sitting beneath a poster that said:

TOP AMERICAN ENTHUSIASMS OF THE WEEK

(PROJECTABLE FOR CANADA AND NORTHERN MEXICO)

MONEY   CRIME
SEX   NOSTALGIA
YOUTH   EATING AND DIETING
DRUGS

He was once again pursuing his favorite dream: to find a television idea that would embody this entire spectrum of

American delights. He had been mulling over a show in which a nostalgic host would pay tripped-out young couples to go backstage and have each other for lunch. That was six of them, but what about crime? If fellatio were only illegal . . . All right, then what about having tripped-out salesmen kidnap wistful teenage hookers from luncheonettes and . . . No, there were probably rough edges to that. Reluctantly he turned his mind to the more prosaic business of a new format for "The Pet Game" that would salute sex with animals, which the Opinion Research people now reported was acceptable to eighty-three percent of Americans over twelve. If he could just get the sodomites to come out of the barn and embrace their sheep on a network show, he would give the sexual revolution a finale to remember.

He was struggling with this idea when into his office came his top assistant, Kwong Sun Lee, a former Viet Cong who had Anglicized his name from Kwong Sun Li after Arnold had hired him to develop an all-Oriental situation comedy that combined cooking, krishna consciousness, and kung fu.

"Arnie, the new Opinion Research figures just came in," Kwong said. "Youth and dieting have both moved up on the charts and nostalgia is down a notch."

"Nostalgia is *down?*" Arnold said.

"Of course: we've run out of memories. There's just nothing left to reminisce about."

"What about those wonderful old nuclear testing years?"

"We're at saturation point with that. Humphrey Bogart, Chubby Checker, and Richard Nixon have all been revived, and interest in them is tailing off."

"Didn't someone bring us a musical about the explosion of the *Hindenburg?*"

"It won't work for the kids. They think the Hindenburg comes from McDonald's."

"The kids!" Arnold said. "It's always the fucking *kids*."

"There *is* one year that's still up for grabs," Kwong said. "Thirteen sixty-three."

"Really?"

"Never reminisced about."

"Gee, thirteen sixty-three . . . Those wonderful carefree days before Vietnam and the Lisbon quake . . . when the whole world was young because the life expectancy was ten." His telephone buzzed and he picked it up. "Yeah."

"Arnie, it's me," Randy said.

"Randy! Where the hell have you *been?* The Pavlov people have been looking all *over* for you!"

"Tell him my schnauzer won't eat liver," Kwong said.

"Arnie, are you sitting down? 'Cause I don't want you to hurt yourself when you hear what I've got to say."

"Yeah, I'm down; go ahead."

"Well, I just happen to have made the second or third greatest discovery of all time: I've found a way to make people *young!* I've found *immortality!"*

"Now listen, kid," Arnold said in the special way he addressed his older brother, "this kind of thing happens to everyone these days, and you're going to be just fine. Just stay away from the windows and tell me where you are."

"With Sidney and Saralee Kravitz at Eighty East End. I've rejuvenated 'em *both*—but don't worry, I'm gonna get around to the rest of the world in a couple of weeks. Get ready to soften all those arteries, boys: I'm taking everybody down!"

Arnold covered the phone with his hand and grimly said to Kwong, "The poor bastard's flipped; male menopause, I think; he's almost forty." Into the phone he said, "All right now, kid, just stay where you are and I'll be right up. All you need is a week or two in the sun with Mom and Dad."

"I'm gonna give Mom and Dad fifty-five for their anniversary.

Hey, Arnie, how'd you like to be fourteen or fifteen again? Wanna go back to those good old days of prom corsages and wet dreams?"

Through the receiver, Arnold now heard, "Who you talking to, sweetie?" and he recognized the voice from a David Susskind discussion of transsexualism for preteens.

"Christ, you *are* with Cupcake Kravitz!" he said.

"And you've got to believe me, Arnie: I made her forty-*three* or maybe even *two* with this stuff I found in the lab; I'll explain it all when we get together. Look, there's a big coming-out party tonight: they're using their new bodies to get him going for President. Come on up here, Arnie; I need your help with this thing."

"That's for certain, kid. Immortality is one thing that has to be packaged right. The Catholics did it and so can we!"

For the rest of the day, while he pretended to be interested in a new genial gynecologist to referee "The Ovary Game," Arnold pondered this incredible turn of events. His own brother had found the Fountain of Youth and for some strange reason was going to use it to put Sidney Kravitz in the White House. That was ridiculous, of course: a much better use of the find would be "The Rejuvenation Game." He could see it all now: week after week, lucky old couples going hand in hand toward their teenage years.

Eight

Whenever Sidney and Saralee Kravitz happened to be together, they dreamed of becoming America's new golden couple. They already had so much brass that on just a single day's notice they were able to book for their coming-out party everyone in the city who mattered except the fire commissioner, two pimps, and the Cardinal. While Randy had gone shopping for more hormones and tonic mix, Saralee had told her dozens of friends that she and the senator just couldn't resist throwing a spur-of-the-moment little bash to aid all the men who were still on death row; and there would also be a very dramatic surprise.

"Some condemned men will be there with those cute little shaved heads?" her friend Bunny Selesnick had asked.

"No, but we're all condemned, aren't we?" Saralee had said. Except me, she'd thought. I've got this death shit licked.

By nine o'clock the Kravitz apartment was already filled with both VIPs and DPs, for three of the guests belonged at a seder across the hall. To accent the theme of the evening, several people were wearing handsome silver bracelets inscribed with the names of men who were still on death row.

By 9:30, forty more people were packed into the great two-story living room, all so absorbed in their own remarks that none of them noticed that the Kravitzes weren't there. Neither was Randy, but only Arnold would have known, and he was still at the office, detained by a crisis over the discovery of a transvestite who had reached the semifinals of "The Ovary Game."

Randy, Sidney, and Saralee all were hiding in the maid's bedroom, awaiting the moment when the pre-golden couple would make their grand descent and dramatically display the new forms that had emerged from a couple of upper-middle-aged cocoons.

"Go on down there and mix now, sweetie," Saralee said to Randy.

"I'd rather stay up here and mix," he told her, unpacking some Schweppes. "I don't know when you two will be needing your booster shots."

"Let him work if he wants," said Sidney, who was standing before a mirror, entranced by a vision of the way he had looked when he had rigged his first election to the House. His age had been reduced as much as Saralee's; but in addition to his firmer muscles, smoother skin, and brighter eyes, a small conflict had developed between his old and new selves on the top of his head: the overnight emergence of genuine hair had sent his transplant into retreat, so that every few minutes a strand or two would abandon his scalp.

"How the hell can I face all those people when I'm moulting?" he said.

"They'll never notice it," said Saralee; "they'll be too stunned by the total effect. Why, I might even have an affair with you."

Randy gazed with jealousy at the renovated Sidney, and then he looked adoringly at Saralee, wondering once again why he had let himself get sucked into an arrangement that was unique in the annals of both biology and romance.

"What are you two going to tell them when they ask how this was done?" Randy said.

"Anything but the truth," said Sidney, advancing his favorite point of view. "This thing *has* to be our secret for now. Sorry about that, Randy, but your credit will come. When I'm elected, I'll get the Swedes to give you the Nobel Prize. I'll trade them some wheat for it."

"Go on out now, sweetie," Saralee said to Randy. "You can't make the entrance with us, and these are people you should get to know. They're the best people, though of course a lot of them stink."

"Okay then, Saralee, good luck." He turned to Sidney and halfheartedly said, "You too."

And then Randy went downstairs and waded into the cream of society.

"A kind of selective, biweekly bombing of Okinawa would make a lot of sense," he heard a hairdresser say. "Sort of a modified protective intervention. The place is full of both former and potential enemies."

"Oh, absolutely," an actress replied. "It would be much better to bomb Okinawa now, while it still has a modest economy, than to wait and have to bomb it when there's so much for us to rebuild. The American taxpayer should get a break in this one."

Randy moved away from them and tuned his antenna to editors Roger Blackman and Dora Dooley Hatch.

"I hear he was once arrested with Cesar Chavez," Blackman said.

"Oh, *marvelous,*" Dora replied.

"It was for drunken driving."

"That's all right, it's the *principle* that counts. I'm for Chavez and *all* the young people, whether they're Spanish or not."

"You know, Susan Sontag said that youth is just a metaphor for happiness."

"Oh, *please,* that's last year's remark."

"Have you seen the latest demographics? The youth of this country are now a bigger unorganized constituency than the prostitutes or the Democrats."

Moving along once again, Randy found himself blocked by two noted novelists who were exchanging endorsements for their forthcoming books.

"I'll call you another Joseph Heller."

"No, there have already been nineteen of him."

"Well, then, who do you want to be another of? You can't just go out as yourself."

"If you call me poignantly comic, I can."

"No, comically poignant has more appeal. With merrily tragic overtones."

"Why not just call yourselves the motherfuckers that you are?" It was Maxine, whose manly laughter rose above the elegant mob.

"Randy!" cried Arnold, fighting his way past an elderly gentleman who seemed to have lost one of his contact lenses in a bosom nearby.

"Arnie!" Randy cried, and a moment later they were

together beside a rumpled sculptor who was telling a girl, "Are you aware that ten thousand brain cells die every single day?"

"What an awful thing for the IQ," she said.

Putting a hand on Randy's shoulder, Arnold said, "Kid, we've gotta go somewhere and talk. I know just how that formula of yours can be used."

"And so do I: make all the poor old people young again and give them a second chance."

"Yeah, that too I guess, but there's a terrific network package I have in mind—look, this is a madhouse; let's go back to my place and talk."

"Arnie, I'm staying here with Saralee. She can teach me so much about charity. What she's done just for clap—"

"But you don't *need* Saralee."

"Well, there's something else . . . I'm nuts about the girl."

"But she's *married.*"

"Just a little bit. And that little bit could be *President.*" He lowered his voice. "Arnie, don't let this get around, but we've already been to bed."

"Which puts you in a group about the size of the Sierra Club. Randy, is *that* what you want? A horizontal position in the Kravitz administration? Schmuck, if this formula is for real, then you can be king of the *world!*"

Their debate was interrupted by four loud chords on the living room piano, where a man in a mauve dinner jacket then began to play "You Make Me Feel So Young" as Sidney and Saralee, arm in arm and with matching smiles, slowly descended the stairs. Waves of shock moved through the crowd, and seven people actually gasped, although one was an asthmatic who had started earlier.

"Is it really *them?*"

"My God, they've transplanted *everything!*"

"It must have cost a *fortune;* I think they've even done the *spine!*"

"It's terribly becoming. Oh, please, I want one, Sam!"

"It must be Gerovital or some of those secret Rumanian glands."

"Maybe it's a *miracle.*"

"No, the Jews have already *had* all their miracles."

When he and Saralee reached the third step from the bottom, Sidney stopped and held up his hand, and the hum of incredulity slowly died.

"My dear friends, it's so very wonderful to see you all," he said in the richly insincere voice that had made him a trusted senator. "I know that Saralee told all of you that this gathering was to be for the benefit of the condemned, but now I have a little surprise. I wish all the condemned the best of luck, of course, but I'm here tonight to tell you that America *itself* cannot be condemned to four more years of an administration whose arteries are as hard as its heart. We are still a young country, my friends . . . in fact, still in our infancy . . . just barely out of our first fetal flowering . . . and therefore we've got to start looking and acting so much younger than we've been. And so I now have the very profound honor to announce that I am a candidate for the presidency of the United States on a platform dedicated to *ending* the generation gap and making us all the children of God that we were meant to be!"

While Sidney continued to talk, using young and youth in a regular rhythm now, Arnold turned to Randy and said, "I absolutely can't *believe* it! Sidney Kravitz was an old *man* and that stuff of yours has—"

"Ssshhh!" Randy told him. "No one's supposed to know that I did it."

"Did what?" said a young woman from NBC.

Nine

It was after the last guest had left and the three of them had gone to bed, ready to celebrate their common youth to the counterpoint of Johnny Carson and Peter Bogdanovich. Because of her attention span, Saralee always liked to have an alternate amusement nearby. For Randy, triangular mating of course was amusement enough, although its geometry was a problem he hadn't solved. As a hymn to cottage cheese came on and the senator removed his socks, Randy made a quick addition of the pieces that he and his partners had to play with: two penises, two breasts, six lips, six hands, a vagina, and three behinds; but how should he begin? As a leader, a follower, or a middle man? He had never even tasted sixty-nine, and the three of them now were geared for a hundred and thirty-eight. A commercial for Leisure Village suddenly reminded him that more of mankind was waiting for him than just the members in this bed, and he silently cursed the weakness that had allowed him to be diverted from eliminating old age on earth. But weren't all the great scientists sometimes ruled by their loins? Even Da Vinci must have taken a break for an occasional choirboy or two.

Saralee was about to start snacking on some lower Sidney when she remembered something she wanted to say.

"I'm afraid the way we looked tonight sort of made everyone forget the condemned. But when you're elected, honey, you can free them to make up for it."

Touched by her confidence in him, Sidney smilingly submerged to her groin, rejoicing in his blessed new lust.

"Did I ever tell you that Sydney is my middle name but with a Y?" Randy called down to him as he sat there and nervously wondered what the hell he was going to do if the only opening for him in this bed was a senatorial one.

"The life span of a director is perilously short," Bogdanovich was saying from the TV set. "That's because we live in a youth-oriented society."

Randy looked away from the busy husband and wife and pondered the director's words.

"It's the same for prostitutes," said a woman named Margot Jerome. "It's all downhill after twenty-two. That's why I'm trying to start this pension and welfare fund. Johnny, there are so many deserving teenagers who should be having their tubes tied up. It's also the whole population thing, if you know what I mean."

"That does it!" cried Randy, jumping out of bed. "I've gotta take the stuff myself! You two go on without me and leave a place where I can slip in. I'll just be gone a minute; I'm giving myself a shot."

"Now wait a second, Randy," said Sidney, surfacing. "We don't want you going too childish on us. We need all of the current you in this campaign."

"I think I'll take half a dose and try for thirty-two. Hell, I *peaked* at thirty-two, but no one knew it."

"Terrific!" said Saralee. "Maybe I'll take some more and meet you there."

"But what about your wanting to be an objective control?" Sidney said.

"I was wrong," Randy told him, "and Bogdanovich and that hooker are right. Why, Einstein never really did anything big after twenty-six, and who knows *what* I might be able to do after Testrogine. I had some help with that one from a dog, but with the next one I'll be on my own, so I've *gotta* get my brain under twenty-nine again. Yeah, it'd better be a full shot."

The closing theme of the "Tonight Show" had given way to the one o'clock news.

"Good evening," said the teenage Eskimo girl, part of a new trend in anchormen. "NBC News has learned from an informed source close to a reliable one that New York's Senator Sidney Kravitz and his wife Saralee have both been rejuvenated by a veterinarian who has made them somewhere between fifteen and thirty years younger with a remarkable new drug."

Randy stopped in the doorway and spun around, while Sidney and Saralee quickly ended their meals and both popped up to stare at the screen.

"It is not known at this time whether the veterinarian has been testing the drug on people so he can use it on animals or whether he's trying to go the other way. All we know for certain is that both the Kravitzes look younger than springtime, although chronologically they are past the first frost. And now here's our science editor, Ray Hendra, with some guesses about what this amazing drug might be. Ray . . ."

"Thanks, Ilaga. The big rejuvenation breakthrough un-
doubtedly is either a derivative of DNA, the extract of an
expectant giraffe, or something else. It is almost certain,
however, that the breakthrough isn't Russian, because the
Russians have been behind us in the rejuvenation race—
unless, of course, you count Rumania as theirs. And even
though Gerovital is illegal in the United States, our counterat-
tack consumption of vitamin E . . ."

Randy stood stunned while Sidney looked at him and said,
"But how the hell do they know about *you?*" He turned to
Saralee. "Dammit, the only way to keep a secret is to have
smaller parties than that. Now the whole—wait a minute . . ."
He looked at Randy again. "It's that *brother* of yours who let it
out!"

"Don't be silly—he doesn't package the *news,*" Randy said,
wondering if Arnold had been rubbing noses with the new
anchorman. "And they still don't know the *formula.*"

"Absolutely," said Saralee. "This'll probably just start a little
run on vitamin E, and it's perfect publicity for launching the
campaign."

"Of course: now why didn't *I* think of that?" Sidney asked
her.

"Because you're not very bright and that's good. There's
tremendous voter identification with a mind like yours. And
also don't forget that every other candidate is getting older
and the voters don't like that. Honey, you're unbeatable."

"Then we'll start the campaign as planned: at that reform
school in Utica. I want the New York voters to see that I
embrace all kinds of youth, no matter how much trouble
they're in."

"In fact, with all those hundred-and-twenty-year-old people

in the Ukraine," the science editor was saying, "the Russians seem to be interested in going the other way."

"What about the Chinese, Ray?" Ilaga said.

"Well, the Chinese may very well be doing some secret work, but their official line is still respect for age, a respect that all of us are naturally suspicious of. Now that this new drug is with us, of course, it is even less likely that America will ever soften its hard line on constipation and broken hips."

"Certainly not if Sidney Kravitz is elected President, Ray, and he declared for the nomination tonight. His platform seems to be a kind of national rejuvenation. If Ponce de Leon were only here today."

"He certainly wanted to be . . ."

"Listen," Randy told Saralee as he started back toward the bed, "you two don't need me; you're on your way. So I'll let you have some of the stuff in case you need booster shots, and then almost *anyone* can give them to you." He turned to the senator. "Just make sure you don't go under thirty-five or they'll hit you with the Constitution."

"I think he's trying to say that he's leaving us," Sidney told Saralee.

"It's just that I'd really like to youth up my parents as soon as I can and also maybe get started with some of the other old folks whose time is running out."

"But, sweetie, I thought we had an *understanding*."

"Well, there's another thing too. Suppose the word got out about the three of us? This kind of triangle could sink your whole campaign."

"Oh no," said Sidney, "this is how young people *live*. Isn't it, Saralee?"

"Of course; nobody still uses even numbers. But if you want to make it conventional, we could add the maid, I guess."

"The truth is I just don't know if I can cope with what we've turned loose. You want secrecy, but if you keep *using* Testrogine . . . well, how the hell are you going to keep from explaining it to everyone?"

"We issue a position paper," Sidney said. "That'll keep it vague enough."

"I don't know; I just don't know. The whole thing shouldn't be launched with a political campaign."

Suddenly Saralee took Randy's hands and placed them on her breasts, where they seemed to feel at home.

"Sweetie, you did promise us a head start before you youthed up anyone else. You've just got to stop being so wishy-washy and changing your mind about things, especially when we finally unveil you as the great scientist that you are."

"Americans don't like leaders who change their minds," Sidney said. "When *I* make a mistake I stand behind it, and then the people always know that they can count on my consistency."

"Like Bangladesh," Saralee said.

"Right; people would lose respect for me if I suddenly came out in favor of recognizing it."

The telephone rang and Saralee answered it, still with Randy at the controls; and now he was asking himself, *Why couldn't that Reuben Rogers have given me a* man? *Either I get this woman out of my system or the world keeps marching toward Clairol and Geritol.*

"Oh, Nancy, don't believe *TV*," Saralee was saying. "There's no magic formula or anything like that. It's just good clean living, that's all."

And then she gave a cheerful little squeeze to the ascending masculinity of the man who had finished things for Ponce de Leon.

Ten

To say that the news spread like the plague is to credit the plague with much more speed than it ever had. Five or ten people in Cremona were immune to the plague, but there was no immunity to the news that eternal youth had come at last to the nation with the teenage heart. From the rock-bound coast of Maine to the oil-soaked shores of California, every American who was over thirty-one suddenly turned away from the making of money, martinis, and love and fiercely demanded to know, *What is this drug and where can I get it?* Most people decided at once that they didn't want to be children again, except for a few in New York who were curious to see if they could get into the Dalton School and a couple of closet thumb-suckers in Beverly Hills.

While all of these many millions, the entire underground society that was Age Watchers Anonymous, were trying to shake the wondrous secret from their doctors, druggists, and astrologers, the leaders of several major organizations were gathering nervously in rooms throughout the United States.

"This is probably a bigger blow to us than either Luther or nuns on The Pill," said the Cardinal, who was already upset enough by having just read an article entitled "The Three Wise Men's IQ: A Reappraisal." "It's the work of the Devil, of course. He just won't stop selling youth."

"It's an awful business," the bishop said. "It's liable to ruin the attendance at Lourdes."

"If only the miracle were one of *ours*."

"Yes, but no one has any idea who this veterinarian *is*. The Kravitzes, of course, are Jewish, and we've drawn from that group before, but even *they* seem to have disappeared."

"With all those journalists camped at their building?"

"There's a theory that they got even younger and slipped away as adolescents, but that seems unlikely to me. The senator's running for President, and the highest a teenager can hope to reach is the House of Representatives."

The Cardinal sighed. "The implications of this discovery are just too terrible to comprehend. The elimination of old age is almost certain to cut down on death and therefore the number of people who are entering heaven."

"But the Lord has never asked us to guarantee the gate, your eminence."

"Yes, perhaps that's true; but I do feel that we're obliged to keep the shipments moving along."

"Then what can we do?"

"Until we get a ruling from Rome, which should certainly come in a decade or two, I'm afraid that our people will have to be forbidden to use the drug. If they want to hold off old age, they'll just have to do it with regular exercise."

"The rhythm method."

"That's correct."

Fifteen hundred miles from this alarmed archdiocese, a group of men were meeting in the conference room of an executive suite. Their clothes were gay, their faces grim.

"Gentlemen," said the president of the Society for Total Involvement in the Fostering of Funerals, "if we lose death, it won't be easy to diversify."

The assembled directors of STIFF indicated their assent.

"We might be able to push embalming fluid at some of the rock concerts," the president said, "but a stopgap measure like that would hardly put us back in the black, the color tradition demands we have."

He paused for dramatic effect, while his audience was silent and the atmosphere heavy with grief.

"To lose all our *naturals* . . . to just have to sit around and wait for mine explosions and suicides . . . well, it boggles the mind."

"Dammit," cried one of the men, jumping to his feet, "I don't mean to get too poetic, but death is part of *life!* Not the best part, perhaps, but there's plenty worse. Who *is* this lousy veterinarian to mess with the natural order of things? Some barnyard Christian Scientist?"

"No one knows," the president said, "but we can probably find him with the Kravitzes wherever they turn up."

"And when we *find* him, what do we do?"

The president smiled. "I wonder if he has a family that would be interested in a tasteful way to bid him goodbye."

A thousand miles to the southwest, in the Royal Rumpus

Room of a place called Seniorville, several solemn physicians were chewing on pipes and fingernails.

"It's a goddam outrage," said a chubby young man in a flowered shirt. "An entire science is being yanked out from under us. And many of us have never known anything *but* geriatrics and the splendid rewards it brings . . . the rewards of caring for people who need so much more than a crummy checkup twice a year. Why, some of us—like *you,* Oscar, and you *too,* Mortimer—have been devoted to treating the aged since the beginning and even *before.*"

"Damn right, Leroy!" Oscar said. "It wasn't so easy to quit medical school and set up practice, but I did. That's how eager I was to be a part of geriatrics, and now something like this comes along!" He suddenly made a fist and slammed it against the wall. "To survive the whole transplant craze, only to be wiped out by some zoological son of a bitch! Well, what the hell are we gonna *do?* Just sit around and watch our patients go back to *pediatrics?* The pediatricians have already *had* one crack at them; the second childhood belongs to *us!*"

After the applause, Leroy said, "Maybe there's an antidote. Something that'll make the eyes fog up and the arteries hard and the colon shut down from time to time."

"But we don't know what the damn thing *is,*" said Mortimer, "and nobody's talking."

"Yes, that's true."

"Senator Kravitz seems to be using this veterinarian as his private physician. It's all very strange. Other jackasses have run for President, but they've never actually used a vet."

"Where are they now?" Leroy said.

"Supposedly hiding somewhere in upper New York; but they'll have to surface soon, 'cause Kravitz is in the primary there and it's hard to campaign from hiding. No one has really done it well since Richard Nixon."

"So I repeat," Oscar said: "What the hell do we do?"

Leroy paused to light his pipe and then he said, "There are obviously just two reasonable courses of action to take; and I kind of think we should try the kidnapping first."

"There are obviously just two reasonable courses of action to take," said a stocky sunburned man in the den of his elegant home five hundred miles from Seniorville. "We either find out what the drug is and mass-produce it, or we don't find out what the drug is and mass-produce it. But we've got to move with speed or the thing'll be grabbed by that Formosan outfit that got its hands on that clitoral cream."

"And we thought the vaginal sprays were the absolute end of the line," a fellow executive said with a smile. "That's a nice little fallout, by the way: this rejuvenation pill will move a lot of women right back *into* vaginal sprays. We could add something called Return to Paradise—or maybe Welcome Back, Baby—to our Heaven Scent division."

"Now wait just a minute here," said another member of the group. "Before we just go stamping out rejuvenation pills— whether they work or not—we'd better take a good hard look at the big picture on this thing. To lose the kind of sales curve we've been enjoying in the senility market, the pill would have to sell for an exorbitant price. Now an exorbitant price makes sense, of course, except that rejuvenation is a one shot—unless it can be made an addiction. Now addiction makes sense, of course, if we can be sure that the drug has only a short-term effect. But we still don't even know what it *is*. Some senator turns up looking like one of his old pictures and everyone suddenly—"

"Look, it's all so damn *academic*," the second man said in disgust. "We couldn't run with the thing if we *had* it: the stinking FDA would have to test it first."

"The FDA can be dealt with," the stocky executive said. "Just look how long we had Grand Tan on the market before we had to remove the kerosene. I'll start taking care of the FDA while you fellows rough out the drug. I don't care what's in it; surprise me. But make sure, of course, that it's buffered."

In his bedroom at the White House, the President of the United States was applying Loving Care to his head and pubic hair, for he was nothing if not a very thorough man. He was, however, not so gay as he usually felt during his periods of turning black; for only moments before, he had been given the news about the Kravitzes by the director of the CIA, whose agency had intercepted a commercial television signal.

"It's certainly the lowest thing I've ever seen in politics," the President told his wife, who was starting to put GO, AMERICA, GO! on a piece of crewel. "You have to go all the way back to that Watergate stuff to equal it. Kravitz'll be the candidate, all right, and he's found the *one* thing that the authors of the Constitution overlooked: reversing your age."

"How old did they say he is?" asked his wife.

"About my age now, but he's heading the *other way;* and so is his bitch of a *wife,* the one the jet setters call Cupcake."

"And also Tart. Say, now *there's* something: what about the rumor that they're both degenerates—if, of course, we can find a tasteful way to spread it around."

"No good, I'm afraid: *everyone's* a degenerate today. Use a rumor like that and too many voters will identify with him; they'll see him as the man in the street."

"All right, then what about trying some anti-Semitism?"

"A possibility, but that's better when it comes from the Jews."

"Then you'll just have to find that veterinarian and get the secret and use it too."

"Yes," said the President thoughtfully, "I guess I'll have to have him picked up and slammed around, or something along those lines. I'd like to do it within the framework of the Constitution if I can. I'm still fond of the Constitution and I like to use it whenever I can."

"It'll be tricky," his wife said. "There are plenty of strict constructionists who'd call a presidential kidnapping corrupt."

"Let me tell you something, Edna, that I thought you understood. Everybody's corrupt. The secret, however, is to be corrupt in a worthy cause. People *expect* that from their leaders, and I don't plan to let them down. We can't have the Kravitzes in the White House no matter *what* we have to do to keep them out. I know Thomas Jefferson liked to get laid, but he never wanted a couple of gland cases to be running the Republic."

And so it went across the land, where fear about the effects of the mysterious miracle was counterbalancing the joy. The joy, of course, was intense, like the scene at the Brighter Twilight Home in Anaheim, where seventy-five residents wanted to run amuck but didn't quite feel up to it, and so they settled for pouring their prune juice into a juniper bush.

However, for each such burst of jubilation, there was somewhere a cloud of concern.

At his desk in the office of the New York *Daily News,* an elderly editor was starting to write, *No matter how good our relations may seem to be with stinky old Russia, we must never allow ourselves to share any youth drug with them. Youth has to remain American.*

In a Greenwich Village apartment at an emergency meeting of NOW, a distinguished lesbian with a cute behind was saying to a solemn group, "It's absolutely the worst thing that the pigs have *ever* thrown at us! Mass rejuvenation would make every nicely dried up sister just a fucking sex object again!"

In Cleveland, a builder of retirement villages began to review his will; in Oakland, a maker of hearing aids gloomily wondered if rock musicians alone could keep him out of the red; and in Indianapolis, an investment banker told an associate, "It'll take the FDA at *least* a year to approve the thing, but the publicity really opens up the market for Gerovital."

"My Bucharest connection can give us all we need," the associate said. "We'll just have to find something very common for bringing it in."

"Okay, we'll bring it in in cocaine."

In his office at Pavlov Pet Cuisine, President Roger Scubbs suddenly sprang to his feet, giving a hairline fracture of the jaw to a shoeshine man below.

"That unknown veterinarian—do you *think* . . . I mean, he's been missing now for two weeks!"

"I don't know, Mr. Scubbs," said the man, slowly rising from the floor. "Do you mind if I get the left one later?"

"It *has* to be him and we've got to get him *back* here even if he won't come! Do you know what a youth drug would mean to all the poor people who have to put their dogs to sleep? Stone has to take care of his own species *first!*"

At the Lake Bluff Countergeriatrics Inn, Reuben Rogers had changed his mind about the value of the discovery after a rebellion by patients who'd dumped Drano into the hormones and muscatel in the silicone. "Your rate of regression *stinks!*"

a meatpacking heiress had shouted at him. "You get us back *faster*, you hear!" Thus encouraged to update his system, Rogers called Arnold Stone.

"You know, he *told* me the formula before he left here," Rogers said, "and I still remember the essence of it. It was . . . oh shit, it was . . . well, either Unguentine and Cocoa Marsh or margarine and Seven Up. At any rate, one ingredient I'm *sure* about—Saralee Kravitz—and she came from my supply, so your brother owes me a share."

"Now listen, Doc," Arnold said, "introducing my brother to the woman who wants to be the first nymphomaniac in the White House is the *reason* this whole business has gotten out of control. He's *trapped* in that goddamn campaign, and he's no jet setter, he's strictly Greyhound bus, so that was no favor, pal."

"Well, it's not my fault if he can't handle himself with women. Either he cuts me in on this thing or I'll call a press conference and say it was *my* stuff that did the job. Both the Kravitzes were here, you know, and it just so happens I was trying some very new stuff myself, a top-secret ionization of Baby Magic and ground rhino horn that I can't really talk about."

"Look, Rogers, get in line with all of the other vultures, okay? I'm about to pull my brother away from the Kravitzes and you and everyone else who's planning to take advantage of him just because he's a schmuck."

For many minutes after he'd hung up, Arnold thought about "The Rejuvenation Game," trying once again to lick the format, while in the Denver headquarters of Population Zero, a dejected young woman was saying, "If old age is on the way out, then it's really all over for us. We either disband or we switch to arthritis."

Eleven

The Utica School for Early Victims of Environment was mostly filled with boys who had rebelled against living in Utica, although five or six of the students had been sick and tired of Troy. On this particular day, however, American history was coming to town and the boys would be helping to launch the campaign of the man intending to be the first President of the United States who was both rejuvenated and Jewish. A Kravitz advance man had been trying to set up the crowd at the school by promising some of the boys either Baby Ruths or eventual jobs in the Kravitz administration if they cheered the senator. Many in the second group had asked for transfer to the first.

The rally was supposed to start at noon; but because the

Kravitzes were finally reappearing for a nation going crazy
with curiosity over them, a nation eager to rampage in search
of the wondrous drug, more than two thousand journalists
were assembled by 10:45. They far outnumbered the boys,
who moved politely among them, picking pockets for credit
cards, although any counting of the press corps did also have
to include the boy who worked for Jack Anderson. Most of
these reporters had spent the last maddening days hunting for
the Kravitzes, who had been hiding under Methodist names at
a nearby Holiday Inn, still holding Randy a prisoner of love,
afraid that he would spread the precious secret if he were
ever allowed out of bed. Such a fear was groundless right now
because Randy was leaning more toward Saralee than toward
escape, especially after she'd taught him how to triple his time
in heat: he was now lasting nearly two minutes. He still had
occasional pangs about not using Testrogine for good old
humanity, but he rationalized by reminding himself that a stiff
dick knows no conscience, some wisdom he remembered
either from Dickens or Jackie Susann.

A few minutes after noon, the sirens of police cars were
suddenly heard: the candidate was arriving with the largest
guard ever given to a man in a New York State primary race. A
few reporters wondered why Saralee wasn't there too, but
most of them just pressed toward the candidate to question
him probingly.

"Senator, how does it feel to be young?"

"Would you call this drug the final solution to the problem of
growing old?"

"When will you tell us the *secret?*"

"Do you plan any future metamorphoses?"

"Are you making any internal changes that we don't know
about?"

"Do you still have your original mind?"

"What's your favorite age?"

"Where is the new *Mrs.* Kravitz?"

"Do you foresee any special problems in implementing a national rejuvenation?"

A few feet from the speaker's stand, Sidney stopped walking and held up his hand with a smile.

"I heard every one of those questions," he said, "and I'll defend to the death your right to ask them, but this thing is too big for ad-libbing."

And then he turned and mounted the stand while twenty teenage girls came merrily mounting from the other side, each one dressed like a New Year's baby, for a diaper was the symbol of the Kravitz campaign; all the workers wore diaper pins. These costumes seemed to cause a certain stirring among the older boys and the heterosexual journalists, especially when the girls put their torsos into the spirit of things in a joyous offering of the campaign song.

> There's a new you coming every day, every day,
> But only if you go with Sidney K!
> There'll be miles and miles of youngness in the U S of A,
> So lead the nation backwards, Sidney K!

When the students finally finished all their cheering and obscene sounds, Sidney raised his arm as if surrendering and said, "My friends and fellow boys . . . Let me start this noble crusade by coming right out with the message that I intend to carry to every shuffleboard court in the land: there is no such thing as a bad boy, because being a boy is *good!* And being a girl is good *too* if you can't be a boy, because that's certainly an alternate way to be young, and America's only chance to be great again is to recapture her youth. What was the golden age of TV? Why, when TV was in its *infancy.* The point, my lads, was so beautifully put by that beloved patriot, Samuel Johnson, who said, 'Life declines after thirty-five.' And so America *has* to regain its old supremacy as the youngest nation on earth, a title that we let slip away from us just after 1810, the one that now belongs to some fifth-rate locality like Malawi or Zambia. Certain tired old middle-agers say that America worships youth. Well, I'm *proud* to be in that cathedral and I want to be its priest, but I won't forget Israel, of course! And I won't forget men like Harold Wren, who'll be able to take his Senate seat in only fifty-six or -seven months. And while Harold is on deck, I'll be fighting like hell for his dream of lowering the voting age to reach the people that this country is all about . . . the people with acne on their faces but the clearest heads around!''

Although Sidney now had a splendid opportunity to end his address, he managed to pass it up and continue talking for ten minutes more, saluting the ancient Eskimos who saved great sums in old-age care by sending their senior citizens on one-way kayak trips.

Saralee might have stayed back in the room in any event, for she was already bored with the campaign; but what held her here right now was panic: she thought she was starting to age again. This morning while she'd been dressing, she had suddenly noticed a barely perceptible descent of her nipples, whose neat right angles seemed to have slipped about a degree. Unfortunately she had no protractor to check it out, but just the fear of falling back into her old march-of-time was enough to make her tell Sidney that she was too sick to go to the school.

"It's my period," she'd said. "I just got the kind of great one that you only get when you're young. You go and knock 'em dead with your speech and Randy'll keep me company."

The moment the the police car had taken Sidney away, Saralee ripped off her bra and cried, "Just *look* at them, Randy! They're starting to sink like leaky rafts!"

"Nonsense, that's strictly your imagination," he said, wondering if it really was. Did a shot last only six days? "Now let's take those lovely things to bed before Sidney comes back with a lot of campaign people who'll make it hard to stay there." Knowing the atmosphere she liked for love, he turned on the television set, where an ale-drinking pitchman was telling a thirsty world, "Once around is all you get!"

"Turn that damn thing off!"

"You want to do it *a capella?*"

Now he knew she was deeply disturbed.

"I don't want to do it at *all* until I clean up this decay; I want another shot. And this time don't cut it with Schweppes; just hormones and Ovaltine neat."

"The sixty-three drugstores were looted by the Fighting Twilighters," a newscaster said as Randy reached the set, "the commando wing of the Varicose Valiants, whose leader said in Phoenix today that the entire operation might be smoother if his guerrillas knew what they were looking for. 'But now that we know that there *is* a drug to take us back,' Sonny G. Dorson said, 'we're not just gonna sit around and wait for some unknown vet to tell us what it is. We have twenty million irregulars over sixty-five and we're ready to march!' "

He turned off the set with the feeling that he alone was undermining the national morale even more than Tokyo Rose or Richard Nixon ever had.

"Christ, what I *started,*" he said. "Look, we've really gotta share this stuff or there's gonna be a *revolution.*"

"Are we talking about a revolution or *me?* I'm becoming a Varicose Valiant myself!"

"Oh come on now, Saralee; I thought we left all the stupidity to Sidney. You've just got to *believe* me: you still look every bit as sensational as you did the night of the party. Hell, you look a lot younger than *I* do."

"Don't *patronize* me!" she cried in a voice that frightened him. "Stop being a jerk and just *look* at me! It's probably happening all *over!*"

In one furious sweep, she tore off her slacks and panties and started a frantic review of her skin.

"Okay, then, if you insist, let's go over things," he said, moving closer to help her examine. "Thighs, absolutely unchanged. . . . Behind, no slippage at all. . . . Breasts, still firm and aligned. I'm no engineer, but both those nipples are coming directly *at* me, Saralee."

"Oh, how the hell can you measure right when you're in love with me!"

He looked at her with a flash of despair, for he suddenly knew that the chances weren't good for their finding a lasting relationship within her marriage to Sidney.

"You're just being hysterical."

"Well, you should feel some of me from the *inside*. My *neck's* starting to shift, I'm *sure* of it!"

"Ridiculous."

"Dammit, Randy, my fucking neck has shifted often enough so I can *tell!*"

"Okay, you want to see *aging?*" he fiercely said.

He whipped out his wallet and removed a picture of himself and his parents that was taken at Amherst on his graduation day, the day he had finally decided he didn't know what he wanted to do with his life.

"Now look up at *me. That,* goddamit, is *aging! That's* degeneration on the march! My head's still back in that picture and I'll be *forty* in just a few weeks!"

And they smiled telepathically.

"Make that twenty-eight," he said.

"Won't you join me in a little shot of yesterday?" she sweetly asked.

"Absolutely, my love. Inventor, heal thyself."

"Whee, it's children's hour again!"

She took a racing dive into the bed, while he quickly went to the little refrigerator, where he took out a bottle labeled YOO-HOO CHOCOLATE DRINK and began to fill a syringe. He had hidden the Testrogine in Yoo-Hoo instead of in gin, hoping to keep the maid at a constant age.

"Did you hear that newscast?" he asked. "People are going crazier and crazier looking for this stuff; and some of those old-timers really could hurt themselves mugging druggists. If we don't release it pretty soon, there'll be no country for Sidney to run."

"Just let us get elected, sweetie. As soon as Sidney's President, he'll turn everybody on."

"You know what tickles me?" he said, putting the Yoo-Hoo away and heading toward her with the loaded syringe. "The way the newscasters keep calling me 'the unknown vet.' It makes me feel like a national shrine."

"You will be, sweetie," she said as she lay sprawled in anticipation of another chronological fix. "Someday millions of people will be putting things on your grave."

"On my *grave?*"

She laughed. "That's right: you're taking the shot. Jesus, it's gonna get crowded. I'd better put some more money in land."

"And I'd better unload some—the plot I've got at Forever Glen—while there's still a market for death. 'Cause once we distribute this stuff . . ."

"I'm so glad you're turning on with me, sweetie. You know, they're starting a big nostalgic revival of 1973, and I'd just love

to know what it was like to be a teenager then with you . . . to
be trying our very first pills and joints and lithium."

"And what about Sidney?"

"We'll have to fix him when he gets back or he'll be as old
as the President soon."

They were startled by the knock on the door.

"Dammit, he's back already," Randy said. "I thought his
speech was longer than that."

"He might have only ad-libbed and then it's shorter 'cause
he has nothing to say."

She got out of bed, put on a robe, and went to the door.

"Who is it?"

"Internal Revenue Service," said a voice from the other
side.

"They make house calls?" she asked Randy.

"Tell 'em you already gave," he said, quickly slipping the
syringe into the back of the television set, for he shrewdly
suspected such credentials. He had never heard of an audit at
a Holiday Inn.

When Saralee opened the door, she found thirteen gentlemen in conservative business suits, nine of whom were
carrying guns, six of which were pointed at associates
because of the crowd.

"Well, at least it's not the IRS," she said.

Twelve

"I'm sorry if we startled you," said the leader of the well-dressed men as they entered the motel room. "Please don't try anything funny or we're liable to start shooting each other."

Three of the men wore little American flags and one wore the flag of Honduras.

"Look," said Saralee with irritation, as if she had been surprised by the American Lepers League or some other unfashionable cause, "my cash is all in New York, so I'll give you a check and then please get the hell out of here."

"Oh, we don't want *money*," the leader said. "Have you seen today's quotation on the dollar? If this were a holdup, we'd take only yen."

"They want our campaign secrets," said Randy nervously, wondering what dramatic move he could make against thirteen men, nine with guns. He tried to remember a movie with a similar situation, but all he could come up with was *A Letter to Three Wives.*

"Not a campaign secret but the secret of the *campaigner,*" the leader said, "if I may be allowed some modest word play to entertain a beautiful lady."

"Horseshit, Charlie," said Saralee. "Just take whatever you want and then get your gun club out of here. You boys really have to keep busy with a thirteen-way split."

"The time has come for introductions. I'm Gaylord Saypo, and my colleagues and I represent several organizations that have decided to tone down the rioting in the streets by manufacturing the youth drug right away. Strictly as a public service."

"*What* organizations? Gambino and Genovese?"

"No, we represent *other* drug houses, the biggest in America: Roth Pharmaceutical, Jackson and Nolan, Hooke Pharmaceutical, Moner–White—I needn't go through them all; suffice it to say that the average American pill lover has always counted on us, so we feel a responsibility to service his urge to be young again; and the looting is also affecting our counter displays. Now the only problem with our starting to make the youth drug right away is we don't know the formula. Of course, a couple of other houses are already making it without the formula, but the FDA may frown on that; it could be Carter's Little Liver Pills all over again."

"They're making it *without* the formula?" Randy said.

"Yes, as a vaginal spray for women and a nasal spray for men. One is called Younger Than Springtime and the other is Adoles Scent."

"Well, I'm afraid that all of *your* houses will just have to stick to marking up penicillin," said Saralee. "The formula's private property. And by the way, my husband will be returning pretty soon, and the moment he comes in here, he'll know there's something wrong."

"Which is why we have to search the place right now," Saypo told her as Randy strained to move his mind into a more useful movie climax than *Gunga Din*, where it was stuck. While the men began to search and Randy fiercely reminisced, Saralee stood seething at the halting of her fix. She was certain that a turkey neck, crow's feet, and God knows what other birds were emerging at this moment as if she were Dorian Gray. She was certain that her beloved body was winging its way toward sixty again; and what heightened her distress was that nine or ten of these men just happened to appeal to her and were seeing her at her worst: making a rocky reentry into upper middle age. For a moment she even considered trying to disarm them all in bed, but the balance wouldn't have worked; she needed Dora Dooley Hatch. One of them was at the refrigerator now. Would he get suspicious if she had a gin and Yoo-Hoo?

Trying to hide her growing despair, she said to Saypo casually, "How did thirteen different drug houses ever get together on something like this?"

"Oh, they've gotten together before at price-fixing time, of course," he said, "though on this one they hired us independently. But then we kept running into each other—mostly at Maxine's—and so we decided to pool the job. And you're lucky we reached you first: a flying squad of ex-boy sopranos and some goons from a Golden Age club are coming after you too."

"And some pediatricians; they can play pretty rough," another man said.

"But we're the ones to handle production, sharing the

patent," Saypo said, "and of course we'll cut you in. We presume your husband will be elected—"

"Unless he OD's and blows the age," the Honduran said.

"—and can smooth things at the FDA. We'd like this to go like aspirin and avoid all those silly tests."

"Go to hell!" she said as if daring him to shoot her, for she had always felt it better to be dead than sixty-one; and she might have chosen a very nasty wound to fifty-nine.

"So you're the unknown vet," said Saypo, deciding to work on Randy, who kept glancing at the wrong side of the television set.

"I'm *not* the unknown vet, I'm the unknown *canine nutritionist,* and I wonder if you boys know all the trouble you're gonna be in."

He tried to say it like Bogart, but it came out as W. C. Fields.

"A cocker's Betty Crocker, eh," said Saypo with a grin. "Okay, Betty, what's the recipe?"

"It's none of your damn business," Randy heard himself say, no doubt to impress Saralee, who probably didn't hear him because she was peering into a mirror at something that frightened her much more than guns.

"Let's just kill him," said one of the men. "Then all we have to snatch is the Kravitz dame, and her husband'll ransom her with the secret."

"You two are holding up American progress," Saypo said. "If we don't find that stuff in another minute . . ." He sighed heavily. "Lord, I wish I were back working for the Republicans or General Foods."

As the men continued their search of the room and Saralee the search of her face, Randy at last stopped trying to save himself with movie plots and turned to something more practical, prayer. Prayer, however, was a tricky transmission for him, because he didn't believe in God; and so what he offered now was a fervently qualified appeal:

> *Dear God, who may not exist,*
> *Get me out of this*
> *And I'll resign from Ethical Culture.*

"I wish you'd stop looking for blackheads and pay more attention to your kidnapping," said Saypo to Saralee.

She didn't answer him but instead kept on searching her face for microscopic cellular change; and watching this escalating anxiety made Randy so annoyed and depressed that he started to think about giving a shot of Testrogine to Donna Reed. His first adventure in the skin trade was becoming a fucking lunatic right before his eyes. She had always been a fucking lunatic, of course, but now the accent was not on the adjective he had known and loved.

The knock at the door startled everyone in the room but Saralee, whose hands had turned to fists as tight as if she were about to take off on an unscheduled Sudanese airline.

"The senator!" said one of the men.

"What'll we *do?*"

"He'll never consider a ransom if he finds her here."

"Now take it easy," Saypo said, going to the door. "If it were Kravitz, he'd be coming with a lot of hullabaloo." And then he called, "Who is it?"

"TV repair," said a voice from the other side.

"There's nothing wrong with the set."

"Don't you think that *I* should be the judge of that?"

"You'd better come back later; we've got some diphtheria in here."

"You want me to send in a doctor?"

"It's not that kind."

"Okay, try to clear it up and I'll be back. This country's television has to be improved."

"Quick thinking, Gaylord," said one of the men.

"It's time to get out of here," Saypo said. "The Avon lady and Jehovah's Witnesses could be next."

He took a piece of motel stationery and quickly wrote:

Dear Senator Kravitz:

If you happen to be looking for the missus, she's with us, the pharmaceutical companies of America who feel that our senior citizens and old people too can no longer be deprived of the blessing of rejuvenation which you are selfishly using for political gain to the exclusion of millions who aren't running for President but are just as deserving of cleaner arteries. That's a lousy sentence, I know, but the pressure of the moment has affected my style. It's also a lousy sentence to keep getting older when another option is open. We will call you here at ten tonight for the secret of the drug and then release your wife or make any other arrangements you'd like.

P.S. In spite of these harsh words, congratulations on your campaign. The presidency should certainly be open to every race and creed except perhaps the Protestants, who so often screw it up.

When he had finished writing these lines, Saypo walked over to Saralee and tapped her gently on the back.

"I'm sorry, Mrs. Kravitz, but since you both refuse to talk, we have no choice and it's time to go. You can take your mirror along."

"No!" she cried, in panic at the thought of leaving the Yoo-Hoo behind for some maid to turn sweet sixteen; and then she flung an arm toward Randy and said, *"He's* the one you want! I'm only a guinea pig!"

Randy stared at her in disgust, suddenly yearning to be kidnapped alone.

In the bushes behind the motel, the mortician dropped to the ground beside his grim-faced comrades in the Right to Death platoon: a militant priest, two fighting gerontologists, and three Population Zero guerrillas.

"They wouldn't let me in, but it's too late anyway," he said. "There's a mob of drug boys in there and I'm sure he's already talked. If we shot him now, it would just be a poetic gesture."

"We may as well face it," one of the guerrillas plaintively said. "Natural death will soon be just a pleasant memory."

"Dammit, I'm going to *miss* it," another guerrilla said. "In spite of all that bilge in Edna St. Vincent Millay, there's something so *right* about natural death."

"And the country'll never survive without it," said the third. "We just can't take up the slack with cholera and tidal waves."

One of the gerontologists put his head in his hands.

"Finished," he said; "it's all finished now. I'm so used to all those wonderful old folks; how can I ever switch? The young don't dig placebos; sugar doesn't turn them on."

For the next few seconds, the entire defeated platoon sat pondering the Doomsday that had come. One of the Population Zeroes clung to thoughts of vaginal foam, while the mortician wondered if obituaries would still be given a separate page or now be run like the shipping news.

And then the older gerontologist said to the priest, "Harry, pray for us."

Harry nodded ecclesiastically.

"Oh, Father," he said, raising his eyes toward the parking lot, "if it be Thy will to cut admissions to Paradise . . ."

In Massillon, Ohio, a man of fifty-nine was marching around his living room while lustily singing to his teenage son:

Coming over,
I'm coming over,
And we'll both be pals
When I'm twenty over there!

"No, Dad, for God's sake, stay on your own side, *please!*" said the badly frightened boy. "Let *me* keep coming to *you.*"

But the father was dreaming of going back not just for filial friendship but for the spring in his legs and the zing in his loins that he had lost along the way.

In San Franciso's Chen Ya Home for the Venerable, Mr. Wally Ling, who was ninety-three years wise, said to a nurse named Li Sun Lo, "Would you respect me as much if I were only eighty-eight?"

"I guess so," said Li Sun Lo. "I look up to just about anything on Social Security."

"That is truly grand to hear," said Wally Ling. "Because I don't know anything now that I didn't know then, except perhaps just this: that Confucius grew no wiser when his prostate went."

And in Jamaica, New York, Keith Lee Markowitz, the first American to reach bar mitzvah at the age of ten, began to deliver his speech, while his aunt gave a joyous squeeze to the arm of the man who was covering the service for *The Guinness Book of Records.*

Thirteen

Saralee was in a trance when Saypo began to lead her to the door; but she had gone just a couple of steps when she suddenly let out a scream in the voice that she had used the last time she'd been fifty-three; and then she tore herself away from him, ran to the refrigerator, and started sucking the bottle of Yoo-Hoo like a baby breaking a fast.

"Why didn't you *say* you were thirsty?" Saypo said. "*That* stuff is poi—"

He fell silent as a galvanized Randy crossed the room in a couple of strides, snatched the bottle away, and then flung it at the wall, where it christened the thermostat and splashed into the rug. Saralee instantly dropped to her knees and sank her face in the tasty stain.

"She's an Arab fanatic!" cried one of the men. "We'll all be killed!"

"Oh, you *bastard,* you *bastard!*" Saralee said to Randy from her chocolaty depths. And then her head snapped up as she remembered. "The *syringe!* The *syringe!* Where'd you put the fucking *syringe?*"

"I just don't see her as a First Lady," another agent said.

"All right," Saypo said to Randy, "what's she on?"

"She *was* on *that!*" he cried, trembling with triumphant defiance as he pointed to the rug. "What you've been *looking* for!"

"The *syringe* . . . the *syringe* . . ."

"Did you men find any syringe?" Saypo asked the group.

"She's delirious," one of them said. "We've torn the room apart. Just give her some Compoz; I've got a sample in the car."

"No, Quiet World," said another. "Compoz is better for nerves during temporary water-retention time."

"They're both short of Femiron's vital postpubescent boost," said a third.

Ignoring the seminar, Saypo gave Randy a long searching look.

"I may as well come right out and ask you in so many words," he said. "Would it do any good to torture you for the formula? I have to admit I'm sort of an Inquisition buff."

"You could *kill* me and I still wouldn't tell you!" Randy fiercely said, looking down in horror at the addict he had loved. "I'm making myself *forget* the goddamn thing this very minute!"

And then he inhaled solemnly and his eyes took on a faraway look as he gazed at the room rates on the back of the door.

"I don't give a damn *what* you or your fucking pharmaceuticals do!" he said, letting fly a word that he rarely ever launched at people who weren't friends. "You can all go *drown* yourselves in the fucking Fountain of Youth! But as for me, give me aging and give me death!"

After a moment during which the only sound was "Let's Make a Deal" in the room next door, all thirteen agents broke into applause.

"Give me aging and give me death," Saypo slowly said, setting his jaw. "It would be pretty hard not to have your blood stirred up by that." He put his hand on Randy's shoulder, which still was trembling a bit. "We may be spies and thieves but we're basically decent men. There *is* too much frenzy for youth, and I'm afraid we spies and thieves have been as guilty as the rest."

"But what'll we tell the companies, Gaylord?" said one of the men.

"That they'll have to go back to trying for the ten-day deodorant."

When the door suddenly opened and Sidney, Arnold, and four campaign aides came walking in, there were twenty-one people in the room, breaking the motel's single-room record of seventeen that had been set for a football party, when Miss Sandra Kimmel had serviced most of the Clinton High School team.

"What the hell is going *on* here?" Sidney said, unable to see Saralee through the crowd but sensing that she was around from her occasional requests for a syringe.

"It's okay, Sidney, it's okay," Randy told him, noticing with shock that he had aged ten years during his speech, a fate that should have belonged only to those who had listened to it.

We really could *have made a fortune with this stuff,* Randy thought. *It's just like stockings and light bulbs: it lasts a couple of weeks.*

"Are any of you here to give money or get my autograph?" Sidney asked of the crowd as Randy and Arnold embraced.

"We came because we're interested in your platform," Saypo told him.

"Yes, and so is all America," Sidney said. "And I think we've got some support in the Bahamas too, which is great because youth has to be much more than just American."

Randy was about to help Saralee up from the floor when she arose, a woman who now looked a little like Rita Hayworth and a little like Gertrude Stein.

"Honey, what *happened?*" Sidney said, rushing to her in dismay.

"My God," said Arnold, stunned by her instant years. "I saw this movie—and the musical too."

"Yes, she's a Shangri-La dropout, I'm afraid," Randy sadly said.

Since the door had been left open, the mortician, Population Zeroes, gerontologists, and the priest were able to come right in, lightening Saralee's mood a bit because the room now resembled one of her parties.

"Which of you are the drug thugs?" one of the gerontologists said.

"Pharmaceutical research specialists," Saypo said with a smile and a bow.

"Well, we just want to congratulate the winners. You bastards beat us to him by a hair."

"We're not really licked, of course," the mortician said. "We'll still find a substitute for death. There's always a synthetic around."

"Oh, but *you* people won," Saypo told them. "He destroyed

all the elixir and won't tell the formula. I was considering a kidnap, but now it looks as though it might be awkward getting away. Messiest job I've ever had."

"*Bravo,* Stone!" the mortician said as all the Right to Deathers came to life and gave Randy their warmest salutes.

"Well *done,* Stone!" said one of the Population Zeroes. "Well *done!*"

"I'm so glad you remembered your Ecclesiastes," said the priest. "A time to get sick and a time to die."

The room now exploded in talk. Randy began defending his grand renunciation to Arnold, while the drug men fell upon him to see if he was working on anything else, like a way to capture the secret of Mexican water; Sidney and Saralee were consoling each other on the bad trip their faces were taking; and the Right to Deathers were merrily trading anecdotes about the Malthusian theory.

While all of them babbled on, Randy kept glancing with a wry little smile at the television set; and then a hand fell on his shoulder.

"Mr. Stone," Saypo said, "would you mind stepping outside with me?"

"Outside with *you?*" Randy told him. "You really kidnap with dedication, don't you?"

"No, you're perfectly safe now; we'll stand just outside the room. You see, there's something very important that I have to tell you in private."

"*Semi*-private," said Arnold as he started with them toward the door.

Fourteen

"It seems your elixir isn't quite ready for the Nobel Prize," Saypo said with a smile to Randy as the two of them and Arnold stood a few feet from the room.

"I'll bet you could still find a way to slip it into mass production," Randy said sardonically. "You could sell it like Contac: continuous action de-aging pills." His voice became a TV announcer's: "Yes, every few minutes, friends, one of these tiny time pills goes off in your arteries and you lose a month and a half."

"Look, that isn't why I've brought you out here."

"Well, I just want you to know that I wasn't kidding back

there in the room. You can tell your company and all the others that the secret is being filed away right beside the secret of where the elephants go to die."

"Nice image, kid," Arnold said. "Elephants have class."

"Mr. Stone," said Saypo firmly, "I am *not* who you think I am." He took a dramatic pause. "And the house I represent isn't a drug house, except when the President's children are there."

"The *President?*" Randy said.

"That's correct; I work for him."

"You're a *double agent?*"

"No, the drug story is just a cover. All along I've been after your secret for the President alone, because his reelection is a matter of national security."

"And those twelve other guys?"

"Campaign volunteers. Oh, one of them did some lobbying for a wrinkle remover last year, but they're here now for the President, because they also feel that it's not the American way for any one candidate to change his body clock. It violates the principle of equal time."

"Well, I'm sorry, Mr. Saypo, but the secret still has to be dead; and Kravitz, as you just saw, is back on standard time, so the President doesn't need it anymore."

"Would you mind telling him that?"

"The *President?*"

"Yes."

"*You* tell him; you're the spy."

"I'd be happy to, but he doesn't trust me. In fact, four of the others are here just to keep an eye on me. But I should think that a talk with the President would be something to tell your children about."

Children, Randy sadly thought. The gifts his mother kept

requesting instead of the frying pans he always sent. How many halves of children had he wasted in Saralee?

"Okay," he said, "I'll talk to him."

"Splendid," Saypo said, and the three of them started walking toward the coffee shop. When they got there, Saypo went to the phone and tried to reverse charges to the President, who wouldn't accept them because he was trying to trim the budget. After finally putting the call on a stolen credit card, Saypo greeted the President, who said, "Have you found him yet?"

"I have him, sir. He won't reveal the secret, but he's agreed to talk to you."

"Fine, put him on—and watch your expense account on this job, Saypo. It was way out of line when you bugged the archdiocese."

"Yes, sir," Saypo said and gave the phone to Randy.

"Hello, Mr. President," Randy said.

"Mr. Stone, I hear that you won't reveal the secret of your drug, even for reasons of national security."

"I thought it was for your reelection."

"That's the same thing: national security happens to be me. I just can't endanger the nation by turning this job over to someone who hasn't had all the experience with it that I've had. Don't you like the way I've grown in office?"

"Yes, I guess so."

"Well, you know we can't count on Sidney Kravitz to grow like that, especially if he's getting younger."

"But you want the drug yourself, so *you'd* be getting younger too."

"But much more responsibly."

"Sir, there's something you have to know. This drug . . . it needs a little work; it's not exactly a perennial yet."

"Well, I still want it. That's a President's job: to lead."

"Believe me, you wouldn't want it if you could see Sidney Kravitz right now."

"There's something *wrong* with him?" the President asked brightly.

"I'd rather not talk about it," said Randy with a rush of pity for Saralee, who was aging like a banana back in the room.

The President paused, and then his face lit up, as if an old friend had just been paroled.

"All right, Mr. Stone," he said, "if you won't give me the secret for my campaign, then maybe you'll help me with something that's almost as big: stopping all this looting, which is bound to start affecting the market. You're really the one who caused it, you know."

"I'll be glad to help," Randy said. "What do you have in mind?"

"You're against rejuvenation now?"

"Even for my own mother."

"Then we'll go on TV together and you can tell the people that. It'll be real public service, but you can mention what Kravitz looks like too."

"*Me* . . . with *you* . . . on *TV?*"

"We can package the *President?*" said Arnold, his head suddenly in the booth.

Fifteen

"Ladies and gentlemen," the announcer solemnly said, "the President of the United States."

The applause sign, fittingly trimmed by Arnold in a bunting of red, white, and blue, began to flash and the audience applauded and waved its shopping bags as the President came out and sat down at a desk in front of a wall that carried his Great Seal. The people in the audience, the first to ever attend a President's televised address, were there because Arnold had felt that their reactions might help to calm the nation, especially if they fell asleep. A few of them weren't fully awake right now, the ones who had just come off their methadone break, and so Arnold reinforced them with some cheering that had been taped at the Sugar Bowl; but because of his deep respect for the President's office, he had refused to consider a laugh track.

"If they laugh at him," he had said, "let it come from their hearts."

When the applause finally stopped, the President took a long earnest look at the teleprompter and said, "My fellow Americans. Four weeks minus seven days ago, one of our countrymen discovered the Fountain of Youth. Now we are engaged in a great civil war and people are running amuck in search of this man's formula. I am well aware, of course, that a certain amount of running amuck is part of the American way: we tear down goalposts and landmarks and on Washington's birthday department stores; but the corner *drug*store is a place we have always cherished. Tear *that* down and you ruin much more than its inventory.

"Now I could come before you tonight and order a freeze to the looting; I could call out the National Guard and send it into the drugstores; but I have never felt that the federal government should meddle in local affairs. And so I'm going to let you hear from the man who has caused it all and who will help you to stop it yourselves at the community level, which is the way Jefferson wanted it. Please give a nice welcome now to Randall Stone."

The applause sign flashed on again and Randy, carrying an eight-ounce bottle of water boldly labeled ESSENCE OF YOUTH, walked onstage to a greeting usually given to civil engineers, even though everyone was glad to be through with the President. The President rose, shook hands with him, and then walked off while Randy nervously sat down and put the bottle on the desk. Upon seeing it the audience began to murmur, and several people woke up.

"Thank you, Mr. President," Randy said as Arnold smiled

from the wings. "My fellow Americans, I am here to make the most important confession of my life."

He paused for effect, while the murmuring continued, drawing glares from the Secret Service.

"Even though I am Jewish," he said, "my real religion has always been the worship of youth."

As these words went out over the air, two hundred and eleven local stations cut him off, some going to black and some to red, white, and blue with a clip of "The Star-Spangled Banner," for none of their program directors wanted to take a chance on offending any viewers who still might feel that the enemy was age. One station in East Texas, feeling that the enemy was both age and the Jews, switched right to its emergency show, an animated salute to the Virgin Mary.

"Three weeks ago," Randy said, picking up the bottle and holding it high, "I accidentally discovered this."

"I'll *take* one!" cried a thin old man who suddenly started down the center aisle, his bony arm pointing the way like Don Quixote's lance.

"I saw it *first,* you son of a bitch!" cried an attractive mother of two as she tried to outflank him by coming down the aisle. She looked about thirty-five but she moved like seventeen.

And within seconds there were nine or ten additional starters in the race for the ESSENCE OF YOUTH. Randy had been in riots before—in Korvette's at Christmas and in the meat department of A&P—but he had never seen people so anxious to get their hands on ginger ale, for Testrogine was a thing of the past. He was wondering if this might not be a splendid time to run, but the police and Secret Service swept over the racers and dragged them away, while Arnold told a production assistant, "Nice little touch. Wish I'd thought of it."

When the theater was quiet again, Randy held up the bottle

and said, "Please *listen* to me, you people! This stuff . . . it lasts only *three weeks*—not even *that*—and then it turns you *insane;* you need it *forever!*"

"I'd like some anyway," said a small chubby woman with light blue hair who was in the second row.

"Madam, you've got to *believe* me, I've just seen what it *does* to people and we—and we just can't let ourselves turn into a nation of *juvenile junkies* who are hooked on something like *this!*"

"It still sounds good to me," she said.

Randy replied by spinning around and hurling the bottle at the wall, where it exploded with a stunning crack while all the youth fans screamed and gasped.

The moment lacked nothing in drama, of course, but it might have had an even better effect on the viewers at home had Randy not hit the President's Seal, causing several Legionnaires to call their stations and threaten his life. Moreover, his use of the phrase "juvenile junkies" when what he really meant was "juvenescence-crazy junkies" offended not only English teachers but also thousands of adolescents who caught the show at downer time.

However, rising above the sloppy syntax was the conviction in Randy's voice as he went on to say, "Do you know why I did that? Why I finally just blew my top? Because I can't stand to see where we're heading. Because I want you all to realize what I've been lucky enough to learn: that the only thing worse than getting older is getting younger. And so, come, let us break down together."

A few people booed, but most of the audience broke into applause, making Randy feel that at last he might be convincing the people to accept the march of time. No more the vacillating dreamer he had been with Saralee, he was now a commanding presence as he sat down again at the desk and began to read from A. L. Alexander's *Treasurehouse of Inspirational Poetry and Prose.* Not everything that he read neatly illustrated his theme, but between "Is, Tomorrow a Myth?" and "Who Loves the Rain?" he said, "The whole point, my friends, is simply this: if you feel you have to be young, then you can never enjoy being old." He wasn't sure that he knew what this meant, but he said it so decisively and the people seemed so impressed that both Arnold and the President smiled knowingly from the wings.

The climax of the speech, though quieter than the moment when the bottle hit the wall, was nonetheless just as dramatic. First Randy gave a deeply moving reading of "I Love Old Things," which he dedicated to the Lincoln Memorial and Sidney Kravitz. As he read, of course, he was thinking of Saralee, wondering if she had learned any lesson from her nightmare in Utica, wondering if she was ready at last to gracefully become a sixty-year-old sex machine. Or would she forever be looking over the rainbow for a syringe?

And then came the crowning moment when Randy raised his eyes and said, "I have told you all tonight what I know in my heart to be true. To renounce and denounce this discovery has been the most difficult act of my life. But I want you all to know that it's a far far better thing I do than I have ever done. Thank you and goodnight."

The applause was so loud and long that Arnold decided against adding the Sugar Bowl.

Since the President had sponsored the speech, Sidney Kravitz asked for equal time, but not right away; and then he and Saralee went off for some in-depth campaigning at the Lake Bluff Countergeriatrics Inn.

"I think it's time to take a good hard look at upper class medical care," Sidney told the press. "It's the one neglected area."

"Have you seen Randall Stone since the speech?" one of the reporters asked Saralee.

She stared at him with a face that had come home to its fifty-eight years.

"Randall who?" she said.

"Randall Stone."

"Gee, I don't *know* any Randall Stone. I know Randall *Jarrell* and Edward *Durell* Stone, but I haven't seen them for a couple of weeks."

Randy's impassioned speech, a milestone in educational TV, didn't instantly stop the great stampede toward rejuvenation, but it did slow it down a bit because millions of people were taken by his sincerity, spontaneity, and violence. Among these were even people who had stopped believing speeches the previous year when the President had told the nation that he hadn't the slightest idea how his personal checking account had been receiving income from the Washington Monument tours. Many other viewers, of course, thought that Randy was just a rogue who wanted to keep the secret for himself; and the moment he had left the air, they reached for their bust creams and vitamin E.

Five days after the speech, however, most of these cynics were also changing their minds and the American lust for youth was on its way back to its usual state. What changed them was a story in *Sunset Review* that came out while Randy was still living in Arnold's apartment, hiding from drug executives, personal managers, and the still unreformed representatives of an angrily aging world.

WASTED ON THE YOUNG

YOUTH DRUG DOESN'T EXIST
Just a Political Placebo

This magazine has learned exclusively that no miraculous rejuvenating drug has ever been discovered for Senator Sidney Kravitz, his wife, or anyone else. The Senator's "rejuvenation" was just a campaign trick done with makeup to shamefully exploit for political gain the great American fear of having birthdays.

Conclusive proof of the hoax is that the Senator and his wife again have turned to conventional rejuvenation at a Countergeriatrics Inn, where Mrs. Kravitz is now considering an experimental replacement of her skin with a permanent press material.

This magazine must repeat its profound belief that no American should ever have to take a drug for age. The disease is youth, but luckily the cure lies within us all.

The two Stone brothers had been laughing over the story when Arnold's telephone rang with a call for Randy from a reporter in television news.

"He isn't here," Arnold said.

"You may as well put him on," the reporter said. "He's not such a big story anymore."

"Okay."

He gave Randy the phone, saying, "TV guy for you."

"Yeah, who is it?" said Randy with irritation.

"Mr. Stone, this is Billy Johns of 'Eyewitness Glee.' All of us here at the show think it would be great fun to get your reaction to the story that there's never been a youth drug at all."

Randy smiled.

"I'm afraid it's true," he said. "But I want you to know this: that I suspected it all along."

"Thanks, Mr. Stone. We'll let you know in a couple of weeks if you're right: the station is taking a poll."

At ten o'clock in the morning on the next to last day of spring, Randy was sitting at his desk in the lab of Pavlov's Pet Cuisine. He again was busy trying to forget a certain junior-senior senator and his age-hopping lady, trying to lose himself in work that suddenly had an enormous appeal: helping a species whose only flaw was its preference in best friends. He was hurt that Saralee had denied knowing him, but he remembered her attention span. A dozen times since the speech he had been tempted to call her, but what would he have said? That you're only as old as you feel? In spite of her refusal to remember him, he wished her well in replacing her skin.

As he polished a new recipe for Pavlov's Puppy Soufflé, Randy was being watched by the nation's best-known beagle, Rhonda, a contented thirteen again, and also by his own face on the cover of *Time*, with his forehead slashed by the words DRAINING THE FOUNTAIN OF YOUTH. The magazine had been published on the same day as the exposé issue of *Sunset Review*, giving people a choice of what really had happened and confusing even Randy himself, whose hold on reality had never been a hammerlock.

But all that fame for him and Rhonda had been more than two weeks ago, an eon in the cellophane life of America, and his mail requesting endorsements, intercourse, and locks of his hair was diminishing every day. People were turning their tiny attentions to new things worth honoring, like The Almost Sons of the Desert, the first eunuch rock group to have captured the nation's heart. In a few days no one would even remember that he had just been chosen the morticians' Man of the Year. The gerontologists, priests, and Zeroes, however, had decided not to honor him because his speech had been merely a vague emotional appeal that had turned the country around for the wrong reasons.

When his telephone rang, he was just starting to wonder if the reason that Little Orphan Annie had never made it to puberty was that she had always been soaked with Ovaltine.

"Randy darling, happy birthday!"

"Mom . . . I completely *forgot.* Jesus, I'm *forty* today."

"But that's okay now, isn't it?" she said. "I mean, your father and I are sixty-five and we're enjoying every minute, except the sinus attacks."

He smiled to hear his mother performing her own rejuvenation, the oral technique that would always be the most popular kind.

"It's nice of you to call me, Mom. It's been a pretty crazy month."

"I just have to tell you again: that was such a wonderful speech. And to be mixed up with the *President;* I'm so proud of you—even if that potion isn't real. Of course, if it *is,* you could give me the recipe because you never said it on TV and they don't seem to have it in *Time* or *Consumer Reports.*"

"Mom, that was the whole *point* of the speech: a secret like that would ruin us."

"Why?"

"Because we'd never know when to stop until we landed in the nursery."

"But couldn't you take it sensibly? On prescription maybe?"

"Listen, I wanted to *give* some to you and Pop all along, but then I—well, believe me, it's just the kind of thing that shouldn't be known."

"Okay, okay. But don't forget it anyway."

He laughed. "I wish I could."

"And you watch out for any more of that kidnapping business, you hear?"

"Oh, there's no danger now. Everyone thinks the whole thing was a hoax."

"You see, I only asked for the recipe because it might make a nice little present for your Uncle Phil, who's starting to tilt a little bit."

"Mom, the whole world is leaning his way. And I'm afraid that's the way it has to be."

"I'll try to keep it in mind. Randy, that Kravitz woman . . . the newspapers said . . . well, *was* there anything between the two of you? Not that it's any of my business, of course, but she's old enough to be your *mother.*"

"Most of the time," he said.

Schoenstein, Ralph
Wasted on the young.